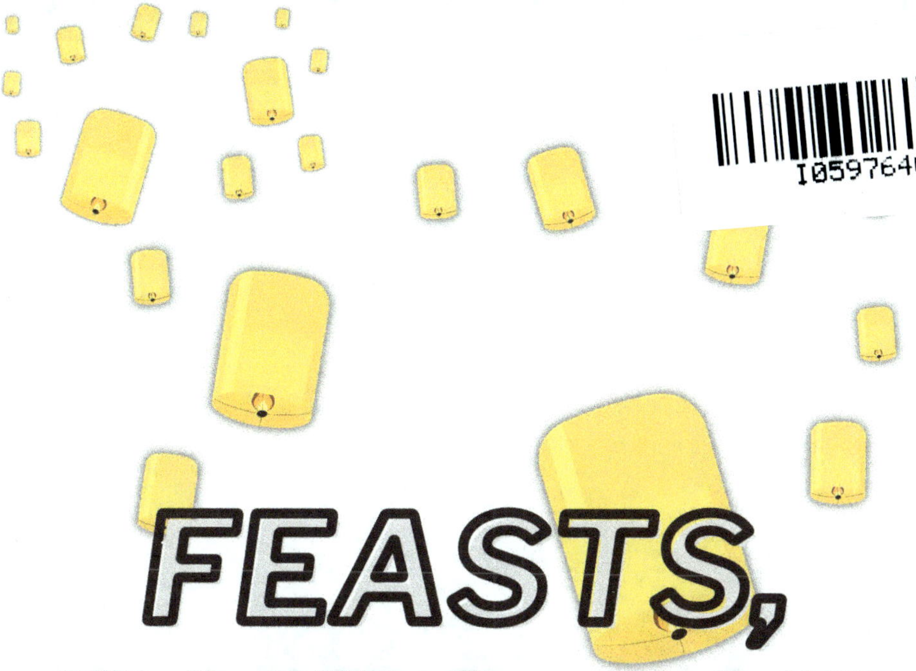

FEASTS, FAIRS, AND FIESTAS

CELEBRATIONS OF THE WORLD

EDITED BY CHRISTINA HOAG

Contents

FOREWORD

A furnace of hot air blew through the bus window as I headed through the desert to Amman, the capital of Jordan, from the ancient city of Petra. A girl sitting next to me, about twelve, asked me if I could practice English with her.

As we went through her limited range of "How are you?" and "What is your name?," her mother turned to me and smiled. We began talking through her daughter. The mother's name was Fatima. She was the same age as me. I had one child, she had four. Her hair was firmly anchored under her hejab. Mine was getting tangled in the window current. She was impressed that I was travelling without husband or children. She was going to a birthday party in Amman and invited me to come along.

I got off the bus with her in a residential area and we walked to a nondescript apartment building. Once we were inside the flat, Fatima took off her hejab, revealing a head of wavy dark hair, polyester pants and a printed top. She indicated that the room on the right was for men, and I was to follow her to the left. It was another sitting room, bare except for wooden chairs placed around the perimeter.

Spicy smells wafted through the air. The kitchen was off the women's room, and full of feminine bustle and chatter as food was prepared. They greeted me with warm smiles as Fatima explained my presence.

After refusing my offer to help, they gave me a glass of tea. I sat on a straight-backed chair and watched a swarm of children chase each other, wail at perceived injustices, get scolded for snatching tidbits of food. I smiled. I could have been at my sister's getting ready for Christmas, Thanksgiving, a birthday or any other holiday.

Not for the first time in my travels, it struck me that we humans are more alike than different. When we strip away the superficial differences of appearance, language and custom, we are all the same. Everyone wants to live a peaceful, fulfilling life with their basic needs met.

Editing this anthology, I was reminded of that incident in that Amman apartment. As I read through the selections, I was transported to a different world with each piece. A rooftop in India, a noisy kitchen in New York, a bustling fair in Malaysia, a pueblo in the Spanish countryside, a snowy sleigh in Denmark, the desert in Israel. Yet, despite the vast variety of places and experiences, I could relate to every piece in some way. That is one of the reasons why books are essential to humanity. They make us see ourselves in others.

A common theme that surfaces in nearly every piece is childhood and family. Celebrations of religious and non-religious persuasion seem to be most vivid in our early years when the intergenerational passing of cultural tradition is the strongest. Holidays serve to bring people together in commemorations of common heritage. On a micro scale, they unite families. On a larger scale, they are a binding agent of cultures, ethnicities and religions. Everyone everywhere has special occasions.

Many of the pieces mention foods associated with a particular holiday. Special dishes seem to be an essential element of tradition, no matter the culture. Even though recipes weren't part of the original anthology plan, I decided to include them as food was such a common theme throughout.

It is my hope that in this fractious, imperfect world, readers of this anthology will learn something new and take away a sense that all our experiences are valuable, no matter who or where we are, that no one belief or way of doing things is superior to another. We should celebrate our differences and value our similarities as both make up the rich vibrant kaleidoscope called the human condition.

Christina Hoag
Editor

And the Rockets' Red Glare

Dee Snider

Fourth of July – United States

The summer I graduated sixth grade was memorable even without the "Great Battle of Ardmore Road" to highlight it. I was twelve years old and still walking tall from being one of the big kids in elementary school, not yet aware of how little I would become again when I started junior high. Since I was almost a teenager, my parents had finally started to let me run my own life. As long as I did my chores and was home exactly at five o'clock for dinner each night, the world—make that *neighborhood*—was pretty much mine. I had a paper route, which meant I always had a couple of bucks in my pocket, so between that, my newfound freedom and my trusty bicycle, I had finally arrived, at what I wasn't exactly sure, but I felt like I was there.

The Great Battle of Ardmore Road is the stuff of legends, and as the years go by, people question the exactness of their recollections. To be honest, there are times even I would doubt my own memory of that fateful Fourth of July if it weren't for all the documentation to back it up. Memories can change, but police reports don't lie.

As long as I could remember, the Murphys and the Niedermans had battled for Independence supremacy. Living directly across the street from the two warring clans gave me a front-row seat to their annual face-off, especially for their final, epic showdown. My family lived dead at the end of the block, at the center of the "T" of a T-shaped intersection. The Niederman family lived diagonally across from us to the right and the Murphys occupied the opposite corner.

My father says at first the two clans were like any other on the block with Fourth of July celebrations complete with the prerequisite burgers, hot dogs, beer, soda, watermelon, aunts, uncles, cousins, a couple of elderly grandparents sitting on folding chairs—and a handful of fireworks. As the years passed, each of the family's displays grew, escalating in competition and fueling a feud to rival the Hatfields and McCoys. Every Fourth, the Murphys and the Niedermans would raise the bar with their pyrotechnic displays, methodically trying to outdo their competition. Other families in the neighborhood didn't bother to shoot off their own fireworks or even go downtown for the annual fire department show. There was no way anyone could compete with the Murphys' and Niedermans' Armageddon-like shows. Besides, where else could you get as close to the action as we were on our own block?

For a certified fireworks junkie like myself (read: average kid), the anticipation of this annual orgy of explosives started the minute June turned the corner and the reality of summer vacation truly sank in. While at the time the appeal of fireworks was purely a gut level thing— they were bright, loud, colorful, forbidden and potentially dangerous —I now see how they mirror the extremes of human passions. From the joyous, most raucous highs to, potentially, the most terrifying lows, pyrotechnics exemplify the chaotic range of emotions human beings are capable of experiencing, and viewing them brings them all out.

Leading up to the big day, every kid in the neighborhood would speculate intensely about what might be in store. The great thing was, no matter how overblown our imaginations got, no matter how apocalyptically perverse our visions became, rarely would they exceed what was presented on the night.

For eleven months out of the year, the Murphy and Niederman children were just like the rest of us; thoroughly involved with all the other street urchins in the neighborhood doing average, stupid stuff. Running around, playing, getting dirty, scratching; you know, kid stuff. Dan Murphy was in my class, and during the year we hung out and played ball after school a lot. Cynthia Niederman was a year younger than me and beautiful. I had a major crush on her, but sixth graders didn't even think of liking fifth graders, who apparently had cooties. Come June, the Niederman and Murphy kids would start to distance themselves from the rest of us and were close-mouthed about what their respective families were planning for the Fourth. No amount of pumping or trickery could get them to divulge what they did or did not know. Their parents had trained them early and well not to disclose a thing for fear of their competitor absconding with their holiday display concepts. From humble beginnings, they had grown to epic Bacchanalian proportions.

Every year, each of the families would come up with an elaborate theme for their presentation, complete with props, sets and costumes to help sell their vision. While war themes were popular, some years the concepts were more ethereal, immortalizing things like birth and spring-time. Other years the families might enact Broadway shows, usually musicals, or spiritual concepts like love. One ill-fated year the Murphys chose the theme "death". Fortunately for them, that was the same year the Niedermans chose the Great Depression, so it was pretty much a cheerless wash.

When the Fourth would finally—and for a kid, painfully slowly—arrive, neighbors from the surrounding blocks lined the streets not just to see the massive fireworks display that night, but to watch the elaborate preparations during the day. Families had Independence Day parties centered around the Murphys' and Niedermans' shows. Rare was the invited guest who would pass up a chance to attend one of these satellite soirees. The Murphys' and Niedermans' annual fireworks extravaganza was the hottest ticket in town.

Construction of the displays started early with set pieces often prefabricated to save time. The suspense among the onlookers would grow in direct proportion to the complexity of the creations being built. It was a sort of foreplay to the upcoming show. Sometimes the orgasmic squeals of delight were so loud, people ran from their houses to see the erection that had elicited such an extreme reaction. (Puns fully intended.)

Surprisingly, with all the fanfare and excitement centered around their homes, the Murphys and Niedermans seemed to derive little pleasure from the experience themselves. What started out as enthusiastic, joyful, holiday festivities had turned into intense, laborious efforts filled with arguing, aggravation, and sometimes tears among the family members due to the stress. Between the competing tribes, suspicious glances and dirty looks were constantly exchanged. To the Murphys and the Niedermans, this had nothing to do with having a good time or the celebration of our nation's birth and everything to do with being the crowd favorite and besting their rival.

Back in the 1960s and 70s, air conditioning was a rare commodity. In the dead of summer, if you wanted to cool off, you either stood in front of the refrigerator with the door open (a move guaranteed to get you punished if your dad or mom caught you), hung out in the supermarket's frozen food section or you went to see a movie. Movie theaters were the one place that always had air conditioning. They had to be. If they didn't have AC, why would anybody pay to go inside a windowless (and back then, smoke-filled) room in the heat?

Since standing in front of an open fridge could be hazardous to your health, hanging out in the supermarket looked suspicious, and going to the movies was for special occasions (or when your dad or mom couldn't stand the heat anymore), summertime was one long sweat with subtle perspiration level changes throughout the day and night.

Each morning, when the sun blasted through the windows quickly turning the upstairs dormer room (basically the attic) into an inferno, you woke up in a puddle of sweat and gasping for air. I'm pretty sure "dormer" is French for "roasting in the summer; freezing in the winter." You'd then spend the day outside, sweating and doing anything you could to get out of the heat and cool off even the slightest. Any kid who had a pool was the most popular kid in the neighborhood, no matter how big of a loser they were the rest of the year. We had a pool. The water was greenish, tepid and definitely peed in, but nobody ever complained.

When the sun finally went down, lowering the mean temperature all of five degrees, you went back into your sweatbox of a house, lay on the couch or carpet, still sweating, and watched TV. When your parents sent you to bed, so they could sweat alone, you tossed and turned until you finally fell asleep in the suffocating heat. Then you'd wake up the next morning, gasping like a beached fish and start the whole nightmare over again. This went on pretty much from July 1st through Labor Day weekend. One, long, brutally sweaty block of time. (Why did we like summer again?)

The summer of the Great Battle of Ardmore Road was particularly hot. A heat wave hit early and stayed long. It seemed like winter ran straight into summer after a brief, but intense rainy season. This made the greenery lusher than usual, which is probably a good thing when you consider all the battle-related fires that resulted that year, but I'm getting ahead of myself. As the big weekend approached, the weather reports predicted that Fourth of July was going to be the hottest on record. When that morning finally dawned, it appeared, unfortunately for once, the weathermen were going to be right.

I was awoken early that morning (in a particularly large pool of sweat) to the sound of firecrackers set off by overanxious merrymakers getting a head start on the festivities. The extreme humidity made the detonations sound like muffled thuds and the cicadas in the trees were already screaming for whatever it is they scream for. But nothing could lessen my enthusiasm for the day and night ahead. This was *the* event of every year, and something told me this year was going to be the mother of them all.

As usual, families had already begun to drag out lawn chairs, chaise lounges, coolers, umbrellas and other accoutrements de summer to secure their bit of asphalt real estate on the street. Some families even ran extension cords and hoses to their spot. Due to my family's prime viewing location, we didn't have to concern ourselves with such mundane efforts. We simply brought everything onto our porch. It was the only time that we were the envy of our neighbors and loathed universally. It felt pretty good.

The occasional scuffle was known to break out during some of the territorial negotiations on the block. Someone would try to monopolize more than their fair share of street or worse, move someone else's belongings to make room for their own. This would result in a yelling match and once in a while some pushing and shoving, not really surprising for an event of this magnitude. But that year there seemed to be more scuffles than usual, and there was even a fist fight, if a few wildly thrown punches that missed their mark before the combatants were pulled apart could be called that. Maybe it was brought on by the tropical heat, but tempers were shorter and nerves unusually frayed. The sounds of sirens somewhere in our town, usually a disregarded accompaniment to the revelry, seemed closer than usual and far more ominous.

Once people had set up their spots, they flocked to the street in front of the rivals' homes to get a closer look at their preparations. Tensions were higher than ever between the Murphys and Niedermans, and among the family members themselves. There had never been any love lost between the two clans, but their animosity was reaching new heights of antagonism—and their fans loved it.

There were Murphy fans and Niederman fans, each capable of justifying their allegiance with detailed points of reference from years past, defending their undying belief that their favorite family put on the best show. Many others, including myself, didn't choose a side but cheered both equally, never really wanting a clear winner. We felt the thrill was in the competition, which would be diminished if one family were to stand clearly above the other.

As the day dragged on, the crowd increased, the temperature and humidity rose, and the Murphys' and Niedermans' constructions grew. One problem quickly became evident: both families had chosen the same theme—*the War of 1812*. Even more unsettling, both presentations mirrored each other. Plywood facades of the U.S.S. Constitution, maps of the Northern Territories and Canada, cutouts of American, British and French soldiers and Indians, and cannons! Each house had a battery of mock cannons, barrels pointed into the sky. If the two families had worked together on a joint presentation, they could not have been more alike. Neither side was pleased about this happenstance. Their resentment for each other was palpable.

The war of words between the Murphys and Niedermans escalated and accusations between clan members flew. Each group was certain someone in their ranks had violated family trust, but to the casual observer it was clear it was an incredible coincidence. Once you chose the War of 1812 as your theme, what else could you construct but, soldiers, Indians, cannons and the U.S.S. Constitution? Besides, while the set design was an important part of the presentation, it was just a facade for the fireworks themselves. That was the real show.

Pyrotechnic deployment is a fine art, requiring timing, a sense of drama, style and finesse. Any amateur can light a fuse and run, but only a master can build a "fireworks spectacular," a rousing audio and visual experience that will ring in the audience's ears and burn in their retinas for days. In the wrong hands even the most professional grade explosives can bore an audience to tears. This was never a concern for the Murphys and Niedermans. If fireworks deployment was awarded belts like in karate, they were tenth degree, grand master, black belts—*with red tips.*

Other points of much conjecture each year were the surprises each family might have in store...and where the hell did they get those damn fireworks? Fireworks were illegal in New York State, yet the feuding families seemed to have a never-ending supply of the contraband and no problem with the authorities. As massive as the yearly fanfare was, there was never any concern about police intervention. Why? Because local law enforcement agents brought *their* families to see the shows. Problem solved. Plus, a couple of our neighbors were volunteer firemen who monitored the event, so a blind eye was conveniently turned. But how the Murphys and Niedermans managed to come up with new, exotic explosives each year was an ongoing mystery. Rumors abounded, especially among us kids. Most of the stories centered around ancient, secret societies (probably Ninjas) who smuggled in the best fireworks from the Far East and delivered the precious black-market cargo to the Murphys and Niedermans under the cover of darkness. My old man, although never much of a conspiracy theorist, swore each year he saw some weird guy in an old station wagon make deliveries to both houses. Then again, what did he know? He thought banning television in our house for a year was a good idea. And why would this weird guy supply *both* families? That would be a conflict of interest, unless he was the one fueling the rivalry between them, which would be in his financial interest. I prefer the Ninjas theory, which I still believe.

Source issues aside, the bottom line was, each year both families always had some spectacular new visual sensation to tantalize the crowd. This was something else for the multitudes to discuss, debate and anticipate with Christmas-like delight.

Throughout that day, the street fair atmosphere continued. Since it became impossible for cars to pass, the town would grant a block party permit and our street was closed to traffic. Music played, children ran from one house to the other (except for the Murphys' and Niedermans'), and adults were carefree and uninhibited, partially due to the massive amounts of alcohol they consumed, but mainly from the general feeling of well-being that came with a day off from work and being freed of daily responsibilities. The Fourth brought out everyone's inner child and a myriad of emotions.

Sometime during the late afternoon, the beehive-like activity at the Murphys and Niedermans tapered off. Their work done, they disappeared from their front yards. This would happen around the same time every year, but that year the quiet seemed eerie, more threatening. The whole neighborhood seemed to feel it. The street party continued, but the atmosphere was definitely more subdued. Something seemed to be afoot.

The final few hours of that day, of every Fourth for that matter, were a nonevent, but that year even more so. The holiday merriment was less inspired and more obligatory, as if everyone was simply going through the motions. Some blamed it on the suffocating heat. The thermometer read 102, but that didn't take into account the soul crushing humidity. But it was more than that. Everyone was aware that it was only a few hours until the main event at 10 p.m. sharp, and nervous tension was building. Traditionally, those last few hours were the time to do things that might later interfere with full enjoyment of the night's display—eating, napping, store runs, bathroom breaks, etc.

The relentless sun had barely dropped below the horizon when many lesser purveyors of the explosive arts in surrounding neighborhoods started setting off their wares. Being amateurs, they had neither the patience nor timing to wait until full darkness...unlike the Murphys and Niedermans. Not so much as a sparkler was ignited on their property, or any of the surrounding homes. Setting off any fireworks in the vicinity of either home was considered a slap in the face to the families. If anyone in the neighborhood wanted to set off their own stash, they went at least several blocks away out of sheer respect.

The Murphys' and the Niedermans' homes were still, silent and dark. Brooding. Their cars weren't on the streets or in their driveways. To the uninitiated, it would appear no one was home.

At precisely 10 p.m. Eastern Standard Time, lights dramatically illuminated the Murphy and Niederman properties. The crowd cheered, and as if on cue, both families emerged from their homes. True to their theme, they were all dressed in period military garb as American soldiers with ranks determined by age, from children dressed as privates up to grandparents who sported general's and admiral's uniforms complete with medals reflecting fictitious battle accomplishments. In the early 1800s, clothing function *not comfort* was a premium, as the heavy wool uniforms proved. While both families looked resplendent, their irritation in the extreme heat and humidity was obvious.

The igniting of the fireworks was done by the senior members of each household, usually the fathers. The implements of detonation varied. The men used cigars they were smoking to light the larger fuses, while the younger members used "punks" to set off the smaller stuff. A punk is a dried out, marsh plant that once ignited, smolders, glows and smells for hours. The really big explosives were triggered electronically.

As was tradition, the Murphy and Niederman clans lined up at the edge of their properties and stared down the opposing family, much like the showdowns in Western movies. The crowd cheered as they approached their property lines, their faces stone masks, but fans quickly went quiet as the face-off began. Someone played the soundtrack from a Sergio Leone spaghetti Western loudly through a home stereo, I think it was "The Harmonica Man," adding to the tremendous suspense. The families stood motionless, only their eyes searching as they waited for someone to make the first move. Like movie gunslingers, someone would trigger the first explosive charge, which would be followed by a counter explosion so close in time that it was virtually impossible to tell which family had gone first. That detail would be much debated later, but for now the show was on, to the crowd's delight. The families quickly took their assigned stations and worked like precision drill teams for the next thirty minutes.

That sweltering, dank summer night, it was a particularly intense display. One family launch an awe-inspiring barrage of sound and color, then the other would counter with an even more sensational salvo. The celebration of our nation's birth was truly done justice that night—*until it started to happen.*

The change was barely perceptible at first, but it soon became apparent that the trajectories of both families' fireworks were shifting. Instructions on every fireworks package dictates that, with the exception of low-level explosives designed for ground effect and mainly used as interim entertainment while bigger stuff is being loaded, all fireworks must be projected at a strict ninety-degree angle to the ground, meaning *straight into the air.* This is for a variety of reasons including full deployment of the explosive, maximum viewing potential and, most importantly, safety. While fireworks may be exciting and beautiful, they are direct descendants of missiles and explosives used during wartime and potentially dangerous to life and limb. Locals still argue over who made the first move that day, but one thing is irrefutable—each side was slowly aiming their volleys at the other.

Instead of deploying directly over the Murphys' and Niedermans' houses, the explosions occurred first over the street, then incrementally over their rival's homes. Soon, spectators were looking *over* the Murphys' and Niedermans' homes to view the result of each launch. As the trajectories got lower and lower, the shots were arching over adjacent blocks. I'm still not sure that most of us in the moment understood the significance of what was happening. We viewed this change as a new, exciting twist, and the Murphys' and Niedermans' way of sharing their display with surrounding streets. But I clearly remember some of the attending firemen on their radios, fully aware of the slippery slope the contest was on. Still the combatants continued to adjust their aim.

Volley after volley was launched, until one particularly intense mortar hit an electric transformer a couple of blocks away. It exploded, caught fire and plunged the entire neighborhood into darkness. The celebration had taken a bizarre turn for the worse...*much worse.* Finally, the idea that something was really wrong seeped in. The crowd's emotion changed from joy to fear in an instant, as the very real threat of harm became apparent. Yet, no one left. We were all frozen in place, like deer in headlights, transfixed by the terrifying beauty of the passion play unraveling before us. Now illuminated only by the fireworks themselves, the battle raged on.

A Niederman mortar shell arced over the Murphys' house and exploded on a roof down the block. The Murphys responded with a shot that caromed off the Niedermans' roof, back into the air, then exploded on a neighbor's car. Now the gloves were completely off. Any possible claim of mistake or misunderstanding was gone, and the battle began in earnest. Family members scrambled to aim their decorative, yet functional cannons point blank at their opponents. The crowd didn't know what to do.

Some people ran for the protective cover of their homes. Others cowered in and behind parked cars and overturned picnic tables, still wanting to watch the exchange. Still others stood their ground in disbelief. Some were frozen in shock and fear.

With the full explosive force of each volley now hitting each house broadside at close range, the destructive power of these missiles was definitely being felt. Some of the shells glanced off the combatants' houses and into neighbor's yards or the street before going off. Others deflected off the houses into the air and exploded close overhead, bathing the area in an eerie, cold light and showers of flaming debris. Some volleys hit their mark, crashing through the windows of the enemy's house and detonating inside, blowing out other windows with a colorful display and igniting fires. Thankfully, the local firemen had been quick to react.

Police and fire sirens sounded as firemen and brave volunteers used whatever they could find to fight the fires large and small all over the neighborhood. Some members of the Murphy and Niederman families grabbed hoses from their gardens to put out the flames, but others kept right on firing at each other. This showdown was years in the making, payback for the endless, imagined indignities each side believed they had suffered at the other's fuse-lighting hands.

The Murphy and Niederman clans snarled, screamed, and howled, while other family members on both sides laughed maniacally. To say that the two families had simply lost it would be an insult to mentally unstable people everywhere. There have since been major psychological studies done on this event and the combating families' apparent psychosis. They have yielded inconclusive results.

While living at the vortex of each year's Fourth of July display had always been the best place to be, that night it was possibly the most dangerous on the block other than on the property of the warring families. While the combatants continued to unload everything they had at each other, many of the broadsides landed in the street in front of my family's house, or dramatically skittered and skimmed into our yard. Using hoses, buckets of water, blankets, and a small household fire extinguisher to put out the flames, my entire family worked frantically to save our home, albeit with an eye still watching the drama.

Now, without exception, every great fireworks display has a finale, a symphonic-like crescendo designed to drive the crowd into a frenzy with sheer shock and awe. Never has any pyrotechnics extravaganza, no matter how small or unprofessional, intentionally ended with a low-level explosion. The best is always saved for last.

The Murphys' and Niedermans' finales were the stuff of kid's dreams, very loud and powerfully explosive dreams. Year after year, the bombast of said finales never disappointed. The two families would unleash their fury and light up the night sky. That year, as fires raged, an electric transformer sputtered, burned and sizzled, authorities scrambled and people cowered, there was a brief pause in the fireworks that gave everyone a moment of hope that the worst was behind us...*then the grand finale to beat them all began.*

When the last barrages commenced, there was no separation of the explosions into beautiful, striking patterns. There were just two, intensely bright, extended flashes of light that outlined every house, car or person, in dramatic, nuclear holocaust-like fashion.

After what felt like the torturous last minutes of a school day, the final firework detonated (no one is sure which family could be credited with the last shot*)*, and the explosive cacophony ended. Though nobody else in my neighborhood saw what I saw, I will swear this until my dying day: From my perfect vantage point, two mushroom clouds rose over the Murphys' and Niedermans' homes into the moonless, night sky.

When the last shrapnel and ash fell to the ground, the smoke cleared, and everyone was sure it was safe, the neighborhood slowly emerged to find the combatant's homes *reduced to smoldering craters.* While fires blazed everywhere, the force of the final blasts had sucked the oxygen out of the air over the warring families' (former) homes, effectively smothering their fires.

Later that night, when all the fires were put out and order, if not electricity, was relatively restored, everyone went to bed thinking we had a fair idea as to the extent of the damage. Man, were we wrong.

The stark reality of any nighttime activity is never fully realized until the unsympathetic light of morning shines. While the mystery of night, the pale cast of moonlight and even halogen streetlights can give a somewhat romantic or mysterious feel to most any nocturnal event, no matter how dire, harsh reality cannot be denied when the sun comes up.

The next morning, I awoke early, not from the heat or excitement or even the annoying sound of the cicadas. As a matter of fact, I was more comfortable than usual because of the nice breeze. *Breeze?* In my dormer bedroom? I sat up to discover that I now had a better view than ever of the Murphys' and Neidermans' properties. An entire corner of my bedroom was missing. My new view was positively panoramic! Then came the cries of shock from my mother, anger from my father and general dismay and disbelief from our neighbors as everyone assessed their destruction. I threw on my clothes and ran downstairs to join the rest of my family.

As my family and our neighbors took stock of the damage to our own houses, a crowd formed where the Murphys' and Niedermans' homes once stood. The initial gatherers were people who lived close enough to have witnessed the onslaught or had heard about the catastrophe. I even sensed in them a sort of perverse joy at our misfortune. These people were long jealous of our living so close to the famed fireworks show. We were too preoccupied with our own woes to take the slightest interest in the troubles of those responsible. But soon the commotion became so great we wandered over to see what the growing clamor was about. Being a kid, I was able to push, crawl and elbow my way through the throng and get right up front and see what everybody was gawking at. Or should I say, wasn't gawking at, because there was nothing there. *Absolutely nothing.*

The explosions and fires were so intense that they had incinerated everything. The houses, including the concrete foundations, had been vaporized! The only thing left were craters that went far below the typical six to ten foot basement depth.

Of course, there was an official investigation of the incident and beyond the obvious conclusions about the motivations for the episode, it was determined that both the Murphys and the Niedermans had surplus fireworks in secret subbasements. When the finales hit, the explosions and fire were powerful enough to reach the storage spaces and ignite the stockpiles.

Neither the Murphys nor the Niedermans were ever heard from again. The sensationalists in the neighborhood believe that they, along with their worldly possessions, had been incinerated and dispersed into the atmosphere along with their final salvos. While it's a romantic thought, it seems unlikely. Some claim they saw both families hastily slip away during the commotion before the finger of blame pointed squarely at the lot of them. Either way, they disappeared.

I won't argue the fact that time takes a toll on memories. It wipes out some completely, while others it alters, twists, and confuses. Some become exaggerated and overblown, ever evolving and contorting with repeated telling. Looking back on that surreal event, while it seems as clear as if it happened yesterday, I have to accept that many years have passed, and the mind plays tricks. But how do you explain the fact that every person who was there that night remembers the same thing? Mass exaggeration? I don't think so. Besides, that wouldn't explain the newspaper articles that exist to this day or the two lots on Ardmore Road that still stand vacant. Well, not exactly vacant. There are two beautiful little parks where the houses once stood, the Murphy and Niederman Parks. Every Fourth of July the neighborhood gathers for fireworks on those very spots. *I hear the theme this year is the War of 1812.*

American Wife

Suzanne Kamata

Obon — Japan

My husband is out dancing.

The name of the dance is "Awa Odori," "Awa" being the ancient name for Tokushima, where we live, and "odori" being Japanese for "dance." Its origins are unclear. Some say it's a fertility rite, others claim it is a celebration of a good harvest. My husband is thinking about none of these things as he dances with his friends of fifteen years. No doubt he is drunk on beer and fellow feeling, absorbed in the revelry of the annual festival of Obon, the honoring of ancestors' spirits.

I am at home alone in our apartment.

I could have gone, too, but I declined by way of protest. I'm demonstrating because while I am welcome to, indeed expected to, celebrate Japanese holidays, my own country's holidays go ignored. When I'd wanted to do something special a month ago for the Fourth of July, Jun had refused. "This is Japan," he said, as if that would explain everything.

When I married Jun, I had a concept of international marriage as the fusion of two cultures, not the elimination of one. True, I'd expected compromises, but on both sides, not just mine.

This time, however, I'm not giving in. I'm not going to budge. I didn't go with him to visit his ancestors' graves, and I am not going to don a cotton yukata and dance in the streets to flute and drum. If he won't meet me halfway on Thanksgiving, Christmas, and Independence Day, then I'll just sit this one out.

* * *

During Obon, the whole family usually gathers at some point. I admit that I did go with Jun to his parents' house where his sister Yukiko and her family, his aunts and uncles and cousins and grandmother were assembled.

Uncle Takahiro said, "Hello. How are you?" in English, and everyone laughed as if he'd told a joke.

I answered politely in Japanese, then my husband's sister pushed her three-year-old toward me. "Go ahead. Say it, Mari-chan," she said, beaming with motherly pride.

Dutifully, Mari recited the litany of English words she had learned since I last saw her: "Horse. Cow. Pig."

Yukiko looked at me expectantly, so I indulged her with words of praise for her daughter. I can see it now. Yukiko will be the worst kind of "education mama," as they call mothers who obsess over their children's school performances here.

"They're teaching English at Mari-chan's nursery school now," Yukiko told me. "A foreigner comes once a week."

Unbidden, Mari launched into a song, "Eensy Weensy Spider," complete with gestures. Though she garbled some of the words, she earned a hearty round of applause from the adults.

Even after seven years, Jun's relatives still don't know how to talk to me. I make them uncomfortable. Sometimes I feel I should apologize for being there, or better yet, just disappear. They have never tried to talk to me about everyday things like popular TV shows, bargain sales at Sogo, the big department store in town, or new recipes. When conversation is flagging, someone usually says to me, "Don't you miss your home? Isn't it hard being so far away?"

"It'll be different after you have children," my friend Maki said. "They'll accept you then."

Maybe, but it looks like children are a long way off for Jun and me. Although we have been married for seven years, we have no kids. Mari was born just nine months after Yukiko and her husband were married. Their second baby – a boy – came along a year later.

We've tried to have children. I know there's nothing wrong with my body because I've been to specialists all over town, but Jun doesn't seem interested in getting checked.

His mother would never believe there was a problem with her son. I heard her whisper to Jun's grandmother once, "It's because she's American."

Jun's grandmother, who doesn't know any better, nodded and said, "Ahh, yes. I've heard that gaijin don't keep the baby in the womb as long as we Japanese do. Gaijin and Japanese can't make babies together."

Jun's mother, who should know better, nodded and said, "Yes, yes. You may be right."

My mother-in-law has also told Jun's grandmother that I'm a lazy wife. In a whisper loud enough for me to hear, she said that sometimes when she drops by our apartment, Jun is loading the clothes into the washing machine! Another time, he was standing at the stove with an apron on, cooking dinner!

"He should have married a Japanese woman," Jun's grandmother said. "A Japanese woman would take care of him."

Jun and I sleep in the same bed. His sister sleeps apart from her husband, in another room with her two children. His parents sleep in the same room, but one sleeps in a bed, the other in a futon on the floor.

Just before we got married, we bought furniture for our apartment. At that time, Jun suggested getting separate beds. He said it was practical. There would be no tussling over sheets, no accidental kicking in the night. I cried because whenever I had thought about marriage, I imagined us sleeping in each other's arms, breathing in unison.

Finally, we got one bed, a "wide double" that we cover with a double wedding ring quilt. It's true that sometimes one of us winds up wrapped in all the sheets while the other one nearly freezes, and sometimes I find myself pinned into an uncomfortable position by Jun's heavy limbs, but I don't care. For me, one of the great joys of this life is waking up close to him, close enough to kiss him and run my hand over his bare chest.

Jun likes carpet and sofas and colonial style houses. I have always admired the simplicity of tatami mats, a few cushions to sit on and sliding paper doors. My ideal room is an empty one, void of unnecessary objects. From studying home decorating magazines in the US, I'd come to believe that in Japan this minimalism was typical. When I arrived, I found that wasn't true at all. Tiny spaces were crammed with every imaginable appliance, Western furnishing, and tacky knickknack from other people's vacations.

Jun likes to live in the Western mode. Like most people of his generation, he rejects tradition, or says he does. He sometimes criticizes Japan, but he will never leave his country. He watches CNN via satellite, eats popcorn and s'mores and coleslaw. He sleeps in a bed and sits on a sofa, and he's married to me, an American.

I met Jun at the high school where I was hired to be an assistant language teacher. He taught physical education, but his English was pretty good. Before the wedding, we talked about living in the United States in a few years, but these days, when I bring it up, Jun brushes off the idea.

"I have lifetime employment here," he says. "If I left, I would lose that, and then what would we do?"

Sometimes, when he's tired or angry, he forgets that this is an international marriage and says, "Why can't you be more Japanese?" I look in the mirror and see what others see: blonde hair, blue eyes, white skin. I can't help but laugh. "Because I'm not Japanese," I say.

Even if I took out Japanese citizenship, changed my name, and acted exactly like a local woman, people would still look at me and say "foreigner." Even if I dyed my hair black, got a tan, wore contact lenses, and had plastic surgery, they would still be able to tell the difference.

At times like these, I look at Jun and say, "If you wanted a Japanese wife, then why did you marry me?" He always replies in the same way. "Because I love you."

My friend Maki didn't marry for love. She chose her husband in the same way that I chose a college, poring over applications and photos. She invited me to help her pick out a suitable candidate. Puzzled, I watched the reject pile become higher and higher and felt sorry for all those men whom Maki didn't want to give a chance.

"This one's too short," she said, tossing an application into the "no" pile.

The next one she picked up went into that stack as well. "He's handsome, but I don't want to marry a farmer. Farmers' wives have to work in the field all the time." She wrinkled her nose and studied her manicured fingernails.

The few who went into the other pile had good jobs with decent salaries, respectable families, and compatible hobbies.

At first, I imagined that all of those men were clamoring to marry Maki after meeting her, but then she told me she'd never met any of them. The profiles had been passed along by a matchmaker. The men were probably going through pictures of women, too, making little stacks.

I thought about all the things that had made me fall in love with Jun, things that you can't tell from a photo or a resume, like the sound of his voice and the sweet strawberry taste of his mouth. I asked her if any of that mattered.

"You fall in love after you get married," Maki said. "You Americans think that life is like a fairy tale, and then you get a divorce when you find out you were wrong."

Maki has been married for two years and has one child. She is still waiting to fall in love with her salaryman husband. She doesn't complain, though. He works for a good company, and she can stay home with their baby or go shopping whenever she feels like it. Sometimes she whispers to me about the possibility of having an affair with an American man.

I can hear the chang-cha-chang-cha-chang of the festival music in the street below, a rhythm that never ceases during the dance. I picture the scene in my mind. The women are in yukata with hats that look like straw paper-plate holders folded over their heads. They wear tabi, white socks with the big toe separate, with geta, wooden sandals. The men don't wear any shoes, just the tabi, which become soiled from the street along with white shorts and happi coats that brush over their hips. They tie bands of cloth called hachimaki around their foreheads.

The women dance with their hands grasping at the air above their heads as if they are picking invisible fruit. With each step, they bend a knee and touch a toe to the pavement, driving the thong between their toes and causing pain.

Sometimes the women join the men's dance. It's freer, bodies are bent over, arms and legs flail. The movements become wilder as the evening wears on, and dancers become drunker. The rhythm beats on. Chang-cha-chang-cha-chang.

When I was a kid in Michigan, we used to have big family picnics on the Fourth of July. My uncles, father and older male cousins played horseshoes. Later everyone would join in a game of volleyball. There was always too much food, and after gorging on fried chicken, potato salad, chocolate cake, and watermelon, we would hold our bulging bellies in agony. Some of the adults would lie down for a nap while my cousins and I poked around in the creek, catching frogs and other slimy creatures.

Around dusk, we would light sparklers under the close supervision of an adult. We waved them in the air, sketching circles with crackling sparks, our faces full of glee.

Later, we'd climb into my uncle's station wagon and drive to the riverside to watch the fireworks. Before the display began, the American flag was raised in a glaring spotlight and "The Star Spangled Banner" blasted out of loudspeakers. We sang, impatient for the show to begin. It always started out with small, single-colored bursts, like chrysanthemums or weeping willows in the sky. Then the bursts got bigger, turning to rainbow blossoms worthy of wonder. The adults oohed and ahhed and we said, "Wow! Look at that!" The grand finale was a flourish of red, white and blue, and an image of the flag we'd sung to earlier. Its shape hung in the sky for just a moment before falling like fairy raindrops and dissolving.

During Obon, there are fireworks, too, but they're not the same. My chest tightens and tears well behind my eyes.

I go to a store nearby, one of the few businesses open during the holiday. The woman at the cash register smiles and greets me when I walk in. I wonder if she'd rather be dancing, and if she has been left behind while her husband parades in the streets.

I pick up a set of sparklers and put them in a basket. I add a cellophane-wrapped wedge of watermelon. This one piece costs more than a whole melon sold on the roadside in Western Michigan where I grew up. Into the basket also goes a package of frozen microwavable fried chicken and canned potato salad.

I pay and go back to the apartment to prepare my feast. Night has already fallen. By the light of the overhanging kitchen lamp, I eat my chicken and potato salad. It's the best meal I've had in a long time.

When the dishes are drying on the rack, I take the package of sparklers and a box of matches onto the balcony. I light them one by one and watch them burn brightly in the darkness. I draw figure eights in the night air, write my name, etch zigzags of light.

When I'm finished, I lean over the railing and sing. I belt out "The Star Spangled Banner," "America, the Beautiful," and "I'm a Yankee Doodle Dandy." My voice is so loud that a dog starts to howl.

I feel better. I go back into the apartment and push the kitchen table to one side. With my back straight and my elbows bent, I reach up as if I am about to pick an apple from a tree. I smile and start to dance. Chang-cha-chang-cha-chang.

Sweet Potato Pie
Suzanne Kamata

Tokushima, the largest city on the island of Shikoku in southern Japan, is famous for its Naruto Kintoki sweet potatoes. They are golden in color and exceptionally sweet. At least once a year, usually in late summer or early fall, I use them to make sweet potato pie.

Ingredients:

1 9-inch pie crust
1 ¼ cups mashed sweet potatoes
½ cup packed brown sugar
2 eggs, lightly beaten
½ cup plain yogurt
¼ cup milk
1 tbsp butter, melted
½ tsp salt
Dash each of cinnamon and nutmeg

DIRECTIONS:

1. Prepare pie crust.
2. Preheat the oven to 350 degrees.
3. Combine sweet potatoes, brown sugar, salt, cinnamon and nutmeg in a bowl and stir well.
4. Lightly beat eggs.
5. Combine eggs, yogurt, milk, and melted butter. Stir till blended.
6. Pour mixture into the pie shell.
7. Bake for 45 minutes, or until a knife inserted in the center comes out clean.
8. You may have to put aluminum foil over the crust to keep it from burning.
9. Serve with whipped cream, ice cream or plain.

Garnets & Pomegranates

Merav Fima

Rosh Hashanah — Israel

I run out of the little stone house and climb onto the swing. My tongue tingles with the sweet and sour taste of the pomegranate arils. I pump my legs so I soar above the pomegranate tree in the centre of my grandparents' garden, my toes grazing its branches on the descent. Leaves, silvery in the moonlight, cascade to the ground like confetti. Ripe red fruits plummet, splitting open as they strike the ground; seeds disperse in every direction, crimson blood stains the earth.

This is pomegranate season. Every year I watch as the tree blossoms with orange flowers, their petals slowly metamorphosing into the coronets crowning the pomegranates that emerge from the buds. Scarlet skin darkens as they grow heavy with seeds and nectar.

As soon as the fruits emerge from their flowers, my grandmother hurries to the backyard. With gentle but expert hands she covers each of the fruits in a paper bag or plastic net to protect it from birds and insects. Savta Shoshanna cherishes the pomegranate tree, says it has ancient roots.

This time of year is special in Ein Kerem, a serene village on the slopes of Jerusalem's hills enlaced with lofty pine trees. Pomegranates ripen, the air becomes fragrant, birds sing as the New Year is ushered in

So moved was I by the sights and scents one autumn that I composed the following verse:

Pomegranates in full bloom weigh down their boughs,
sway in the breeze, offering passers-by their luscious flesh,
seeding six-hundred-and-thirteen blessings for the new year.

Like most of my early poems, it found a home in my drawer.

The swing rises higher and faster as the pendulum-like motion lulls my racing mind. I close my eyes, inebriated by the scent. I love the garden at twilight, when the aroma of the roses is amplified. It is as though, when sight is compromised by the diminishing daylight, the sense of smell is heightened, and the garden takes on a new dimension. As though the bright petals have worked hard all day to absorb the sunlight and produce their enchanting fragrance then release it into the fresh, starlit night. Or, perhaps, as the workday comes to a close, fewer vehicles are on the road and the air is not as polluted with toxic emissions. More space is left to be filled with the scent of roses, emitting their last redolent breath before folding their petals into a tight fist and falling into a pleasant slumber.

My grandmother planted rose shrubs along the garden's edge as a living fence, the thorns providing natural protection against wild dogs, jackals, and robbers from the neighbouring villages. Upon acquiring the house from the newly established State of Israel, she found a dry, gnarled branch lying close to the parched ground in the corner of the terraced garden. She pruned and germinated it, replanted its seeds along the garden's perimeter.

It drew the attention of horticulturalists, who determined that it is two-thousand years old, dating back to the Second Temple Period, when a Jewish agricultural settlement thrived in the area. The terrace structure has remained intact over the centuries, though the house's previous tenants neglected the roses and put all of their energies into the fruit trees and vegetable garden.

That single rose shrub that my grandmother found overcame years of neglect and continued pushing its way through the rocky earth every autumn, a lone remnant of the sovereign Jewish community before its expulsion by the Romans. The scientists even claimed that this is the exact genus of rose mentioned in the biblical *Song of Songs*, the same that was later introduced to Europe by the Crusaders.

Now, six decades later, the roses have grown to majestic proportions, delineating the modest property with pink, red, and white blossoms atop long, graceful stems. But let there be no mistake, they are a vicious *Rosaceae* species. Whoever comes near, does so at their own risk.

Once, as a child, I was playing catch in the garden with my brother Hod. He threw the ball so hard that it rolled into the rosebush. I reached my hand in to retrieve it and, to this day, I have a lump where the thorn penetrated my palm.

"You have now earnestly earned the title of '*la rosa entre los espinos*,' as Savta Shoshanna likes to call you," my brother joked, but I did not appreciate his humour. Even now, when someone extends a hand to shake mine, I am hesitant to reciprocate, afraid that they may be discomfited by the slight protrusion below my thumb.

For many years, I collected Savta Shoshanna's rose petals that had fallen to the ground; those left over after she had collected the choicest petals for the purpose of making rosewater, which she uses both as a facial toner and to flavour baked goods. I believe that this is the secret to her taut, radiant skin, even at the advanced age of seventy-eight. She would rise at dawn to collect the freshest, most fragrant petals still moist with dew. I remain mesmerised by the alchemy of making rosewater, soaking the petals in distilled water and then simmering them on the stovetop for a minimum of three hours. She vigilantly watched the pot, occasionally stirring. The entire house would be suffused with an aromatic balm.

I would collect the petals caught in the state between living, breathing blossoms and dead leaves, their vivid red colour just fading. I dried the petals between the pages of Marcel Proust's *À la recherche du temps perdu*, the only one of my volumes thick enough to flatten the leaves. I retrieved them two months later to create laminated bookmarks with the dried, heart-shaped petals on one side – thin and delicate, almost translucent, threatening to crumble between my fingertips, purple veins protruding, robbed of their intoxicating scent – and verses by Zelda the Poetess on the other:

Every rose is an island
Of the promised peace,
Of the eternal peace.

I would gift these bookmarks to fellow book lovers, but I have not made any more bookmarks since my lover Soli's return to his home country. Soli's bookmark was inscribed with a different set of verses:

His caresses are a wall of love
Almond blossoms are his caresses.

I wonder if he has kept it.

A bouquet of roses always adorns my grandparents' dining table, a different combination each time I visit. Tonight, all of the roses are white.

The swing continues its upward surge, hypnotising me with the meagre moonlight penetrating my closed eyelids. My neck relaxes and my long hair flies back. The sweet Kiddush wine I sipped at the start of the Rosh Hashanah dinner makes me lightheaded. I let go of the cords to rub my burning eyes and a gleaming ray of moonlight splits into the seven colours of the spectrum as it traverses the salt crystals forming in the corners of my eyes. Pastel specks dance before me until they reconvene into a white glow as the swing descends. I am overwhelmed by the glorious scent of roses.

Having released my grip, I crash down on the ground. I yelp and rub my tailbone. My forefinger traces the geometric cracks in the earth, hard after months of drought. The swing oscillates weightlessly above my head, its ropes twisting and untwisting, until it comes to a standstill.

Savta Shoshanna runs out of the house, followed by my mother. As always, my grandmother looks regal in her holiday finery, a satin gown and turban wrapped around her head. Gathering me into their arms and helping me to my feet, my mother says: "There you are, Kitra, I was wondering where you had gone."

I lean against their shoulders as they walk me back into the house and arrange me on the couch, propping my legs on purple silk cushions embroidered with silver floss.

"I fell off the swing. The Kiddush wine must have made me drowsy."

My mother returns a minute later, handing me a glass of water and shoving a white
pill into my mouth. "Drink this," she orders, "it will reduce the inflammation."

"What is it?"

"Nurofen." I twist my nose and swallow the bitter pill, though I prefer my grandmother's natural remedies.

Savta Shoshanna reappears, carrying a steaming mug of homegrown lemongrass tea. Her fingertips are stained yellow. I know she has made a remedy. She lifts my burgundy velveteen dress and rubs a pomade of crushed ginger and turmeric roots on my lower back, supporting my head as she offers me the tea. It is sweet with honey. I can see my father, grandfather, siblings, and cousins crowding around the entrance to the sitting room, but my grandmother waves them off. "Let her rest," she says, then turns to me with an inquisitive gaze. "Tell me what's bothering you, *querida* Kitra. I noticed that you are not yourself ever since you walked in here this afternoon. Your eyes have turned green as they do whenever you've been crying."

I had not been able to conceal my swollen eyes as I helped my grandmother release the bright red pomegranate seeds from their delicate white envelopes, filling the bowl with scarlet jewels for the evening's festivities. Even now I find it difficult to articulate my sorrow, except to say that someone I love is on the verge of death.

Earlier this morning, I find Bina's gallery door locked. She has never been absent from the gallery. I make my way to her house around the corner, a stone building overlooking a central square in the Old City of Jerusalem.

When she does not answer my knock, I push the door open and find her lying in bed, covered in a patchwork quilt despite the suffocating heat of late summer. Her slight body seems to have dissolved into the linens. Her eyes brighten as I approach and kiss her sunken cheek. Her breathing is laboured, and she is unable to form her habitual smile. With great effort, she greets me, "Shalom."

She gestures at a stool at her bedside. I collapse onto it and take her outstretched hand.

"Kitra?"

"Yes. Is there anything I can do for you?"

"Read me a poem."

I pull a scrap of paper out of my purse. "It's called 'Adoration.' It was inspired by Diego Velázquez's painting *The Toilet of Venus*."

I had just seen the painting, which is also known as the *Rokeby Venus*, at the National Gallery in London on my last research trip to Europe. I initially flew to Spain seeking access to the Royal Spanish Archives in Madrid. I was hoping to uncover a manuscript by an unknown medieval woman poet but was told that admission is prioritised for Spanish citizens, so my dissertation in Medieval Hebrew Literature is now stalled. I recite:

Her beauty alone she adores;
Veiled by the red curtain,
Bare back turned to you, blocking
You out of her heart chambers.

My vision blurs with welling tears and my voice trails off.

"Thank you, Kitra." Bina retrieves a pearl and garnet bracelet from the bedside table and thrusts it into my hand, folding her fingers over my fist.

"I want you to have this, Kitra, it will give you the confidence to pursue your path."

"Why me?"

"I have no daughter of my own." Her soft voice dissipates then returns. "It would have been cruel to impose this fate on any child. You have been like a daughter to me."

She closes her eyes and falls asleep. Striving to control the tremor in my hand, I fasten the bracelet on my wrist, but the clasp is loose, and the thread of beads almost slides off my wrist. I'm afraid that it will fall off and that I will lose it forever, so I throw the bracelet deep into my purse, vowing to get it fixed. I kiss Bina's ashen cheek and head to the door.

I have known Bina for over a decade since I was eighteen. My grandparents were about to celebrate their golden anniversary and I went shopping for a present. I wandered into the Old City through Zion Gate and walked the narrow cobblestone alleys to the Cardo, the Roman marketplace at the heart of the Jewish Quarter, surrounded by ornate classical columns. The cream-coloured Jerusalem stone refracted the golden sunlight striking the ancient buildings. I knew I would recognise the ideal gift when I saw it.

I soon stumbled upon a small gallery – wedged between a jeweller's studio and a ceramics cooperative – with bold abstract paintings flanking the arched doorway. Bells chimed as I entered. My eyes jumped from canvas to canvas of vividly coloured birds in flight, until I was drawn to a lone painting on the opposite wall of the gallery that differed in its small scale and subdued tone from all the others. Framed in silver, it depicted a pomegranate tree with luscious red fruit and a pair of white doves nestled in its branches. This was the gift. I knew how my grandmother relished her pomegranate tree and couldn't help but think of the doves as my grandparents, eternally faithful in their love for one another.

I thought that the gallery was vacant, but as I examined the painting, a woman waltzed across the floor. Her long blond hair illumined her face like sunbeams. She lit up the dim space with every step.

"Isn't it beautiful?" she said. "It's one of my favourites."

"Yes, it is magnificent. I am looking for a gift for my grandparents' fiftieth anniversary. They will love its elegant simplicity."

"I'm sure they will. Do you know that the painting contains the entire *Song of Songs*?"

My heart skipped. I hadn't noticed. I took a step forward and observed the work up close. I could now see the jagged lines delineating the leaves, birds, and branches consisted of miniscule Hebrew script in coloured ink, meticulous work that must have taken days of concentration to complete.

I read the words constituting the round red fruits topped with coronets:

*Let us rise and head to the vineyards to see if the vine has budded,
if the vine-blossom has opened, if the pomegranates have flowered;
there I will give you my love.*

A shiver ran down my spine. There could not be a more perfect gift.

The woman extended her hand. "I am Bina Ravel, by the way. What's your name?"

I hesitated, but somehow knew I could trust her. "Kitra Vardi." An electrifying energy emanated from her fingertips as we shook hands.

"Kitra Vardi is a wonderful name for a poet," she exclaimed. "Why don't you come back here tomorrow evening? I will be hosting a gathering of artists and writers and would like to introduce you to them. I will have the painting wrapped and ready for you to take to your grandparents then."

Ever since reading Proust's *À la recherche*, I had dreamt of joining a literary salon and engaging with other writers and artists, and now a woman I'd just met was inviting me to hers.

She pirouetted across the room to another customer, her sequined bell sleeves swirling like spread wings. I did not know how she had intuited my most profound desire to become a poet, but it was then that I started taking my ambition seriously and cherishing the uniqueness of my name Kitra. Until then, my name had been the source of tremendous grief and countless taunts by classmates mocking its Aramaic origin.

I soon became a regular visitor to Bina's gallery, bringing her scattered verses and polished poems to read. It was at her salon that I first read my poetry in public. Bina declared that poetry is an oral form, that a poem only attains completion when it is read aloud. "Do it justice by reading it evocatively, with passion." Bina exemplified this passion with her every gesture. Indeed, any day in which she didn't laugh, dance, or sing was a day wasted.

When I first started visiting her studio, Bina was a prolific painter. Her paintbrush swirled in her hand as she masterfully splattered colour on canvas. But over the ten years of our friendship, Bina's health deteriorated, until she could no longer hold a brush. First her wrist started shaking and her lines became uneven. She suffered immense pain when she attempted to unclasp her fist and release the brush. Then her eyes glazed over with a thick layer of cataracts and her paintings grew sombre. It was unclear what she was suffering from, and she never said.

She finally had to give up painting and devoted herself to nurturing younger artists, featuring their work in her gallery. She did it with such enthusiasm and grace that I never suspected that her condition was fatal.

Until that morning.

———————

Bina's painting of the pomegranate tree hangs on a prominent wall in my grandparents' living room and I admire it now as I recline on the sofa, rubbing my sore back.

"I know how important Bina has been to you," my mother begins, holding me in a tight embrace. "I am sorry to be the bearer of bad news, but it sounds like she is suffering from myotonic dystrophy."

"Myotonic what?"

"Myotonic dystrophy. It's a degenerative disease that affects the nervous system, before attacking the heart and respiratory system."

"How did she get it? Is it contagious?"

"It's a hereditary disease, common among Sephardic Jews."

"What makes you think that she is Sephardic? She has blond hair, and her skin is fairer than mine."

Rising from the sofa, my mother taps the bottom corner of the painting's glass frame with her manicured fingernail. "Bina signs her work 'Bina Ravel ST'."

"Isn't ST an abbreviation for 'Saint'? Maybe her mother had an affair with an English officer during the British Mandate?"

"No, ST stands for *Sephardi Tahor*, 'Pure-blooded Sephardic.' STs are so proud of their Spanish heritage that they only marry amongst themselves. That's why hereditary diseases, such as myotonic dystrophy, grow more severe with every generation."

An image of Bina subsumed under her quilt fills my mind. "Is it hopeless then? Can anything be done to help her?"

"As a physician, I can tell you that there is no known cure. I am so sorry, Kitra."

I bury my face in the embroidered cushions strewn on the sofa and taste saltwater on the tip of my tongue.

———————

"Eat this, *querida* Kitra, it will help you recover your strength." Supporting my head in the crook of her elbow, Savta Shoshanna gives me a spoonful of her specialty, date salad with kumquats and almonds, marinated in rosewater, honey, and orange nectar and seasoned with a dash of cinnamon. As I chew, I am reinvigorated by the sweetness.

"Come join us at the table. We've been waiting for you to move on to the main part of the feast. We haven't yet blessed the bread." My grandfather pulls at the corner of the embroidered silk *hallah* cover to reveal two round loaves of bread atop a pristine white tablecloth.

"*Madre*, how many times do I have to tell you that white flour is unhealthy?" my mother says. "Why do you insist on baking white *hallah*? Wholemeal or rye would be much more nutritious, particularly given your high blood sugar level."

"*Querida* Rachel, I am sorry, but we simply cannot recite the blessing over bread made with unrefined flour," Savta Shoshanna says. "The *Zohar* specifically states that the chaff is like the *kelipot*, the peels of evil in which the divine spirit is trapped. It is up to us to release it to its heavenly abode. Besides, it won't kill me to eat refined flour once in a while."

"Not to mention that this isn't a regular round *hallah*, Rachel," Sabba Yedidya, my grandfather, says, as he pulls apart the loaf and distributes the morsels dipped in honey to everyone around the table. "Your mother worked very hard to shape the bread into a thirteen-petalled rose, the family emblem."

"Family emblem? I've never heard of a family emblem," Sarah, my mother's younger sister, says from the other end of the table.

"The rose has been symbolic to our family for many generations," Savta Shoshanna says. "That's why I chose the surname Vardi when I arrived in Israel in 1948. Vardi means 'roselike.'"

Turning to my mother, my grandfather says, "I see that you have chosen to keep the surname Vardi and pass it on to your children."

"That's because Maor's surname – Katoschevski – is next to unpronounceable."

My father nods. "When we first met, Rachel was too embarrassed to introduce me to her friends, because no one could pronounce my surname. When I was appointed commander of the Air Force base, I had to choose a Hebrew surname, so I took Vardi."

"Exactly, Vardi is a proper Israeli name," my mother says with pride.

"Is that why I was given such an unusual first name?" I recover my voice. "I can't tell you the number of times I was ridiculed for having such an archaic name."

"Growing up in this family," my mother says, "it was clear to me that I would name my firstborn daughter after the highest *sefira*. I didn't want you to be just any crown – Keter – but *the* crown. The final *aleph* in the Aramaic form of Kitra gives it that added distinctiveness. Then Hod was born, and your twin sisters, Tiferet and Ateret. They are also named after the *sefirot*."

"At least they've got Hebrew names."

"Family legend has it that you have royal blood. A distinguished name like Kitra seems to me quite appropriate for such a special person as yourself," my mother says. "You are destined for greatness."

I look around the table at the faces of my family and smile. My gaze pauses at my nephew Oshri, his blond curls falling over his almond-shaped blue eyes. How he has grown in the two years since his birth. I remember when my brother Hod had his first child, the family gathered around this same table on the seventh night following his birth, the night before he was to be circumcised, for the *Leil HaZohar* ceremony. Oshri was my grandparents' first great-grandchild and Savta Shoshanna outdid herself for the occasion, spending the entire week in the kitchen baking pastries from family recipes that had been handed down from mother to daughter for hundreds of years. As my mother was hopeless in the kitchen, so she declared, it was my turn to be initiated into those culinary secrets.

My grandmother's pastries were savoury, rather than sweet, and melted in your mouth when dipped in tea, but no matter how hard I tried, my batches came out so bland and dry to the point of being inedible.

As the eldest of my siblings, everyone expected me to be the first to get married, but Hod beat me to it. He met the love of his life on his post-army trip to South America and they married while still in university. I, on the other hand, still have no prospect of a husband.

The night of the *Leil HaZohar*, we sat around the long table, taking turns reciting passages of the *Zohar* from an old, tattered, leather-bound book. Though none of us understood the Aramaic, except for the occasional word resembling the Hebrew root, we read with fervent devotion, praying that the sacred words would protect the newborn from Lilith and the demons seeking to inflict harm on his body and soul as the *mohel* sliced his foreskin the next morning.

This ceremony was a sacred custom in our family. I have never heard of it anywhere else. As we recited the Aramaic verses, I could see the guardian angels donning translucent gowns of white light, their iridescent wings fluttering as they hovered around the table.

My sister Ateret reaches for the wine bottle. "More wine or would you prefer *arak*?"

"Wait." My mother holds up her hand. "Don't give her any more alcohol. She just took Nurofen."

My father's chair scrapes the floor as he suddenly rises from the table, tall and handsome in his pressed beige uniform. "I must get back to the base now. I was just waiting to see how you are feeling, Kitra. Take care of yourself. *Shana Tova* everyone!" He kisses the top of my head and departs.

Delectable smells fill the house as the main course is served – Savta Shoshanna's famous lamb tagine with dried fruits, walnuts, and caramelised onions seasoned with cinnamon, cardamom, and cloves, rice with slivered almonds and raisins, and a bulgur salad dressed with pomegranate vinaigrette, freshly extracted from the fruit of the tree in the garden. These are the dishes I crave whenever I visit my grandparents, but I have lost my appetite to the throbbing pain in my back. My eyes shut as I return to the sofa and sink into the cushions.

I awaken to the sound of porcelain clacking as dishes are washed, dried, and put away by a well-trained assembly line of young cousins, albeit with a slight delay where I should have been stationed. Sabba Yedidya extends his right hand to be kissed by each of his children and grandchildren, before saying good night and going to bed.

"You really mustn't drive home tonight in your state, Kitra," Savta Shoshanna says. "Spend the night here with us."

"Your grandmother's right," my mother says. "I'm sorry I can't drive you home. I need to get going now before I'm late for my shift at the hospital."

Once all of the guests have left, Savta Shoshanna collapses onto the rocking chair next to the couch, exhausted.

"I have a Rosh Hashana present for you, *querida* Kitra," she says. "I think it's time you had this."

She reaches her hands behind her nape, unclasps the chain and secures it around my neck. For as long as I can remember, my grandmother has worn this gold chain, with a pomegranate-shaped pendant. Its scarlet jewels – garnets, my birthstone – emit an unusual radiance. As a child curled in her lap, I couldn't resist handling it, my fingers drawn to its cool, smooth surface like metal to magnet. Turning the pendant over in my palm, I would ask, "What does it say here?" She would recite the engraved verses:

My beloved is a locked garden, a sealed fountain;
A pomegranate orchard with exquisite fruits.

She never let me try it on, no matter how much I implored.

"This necklace has been in the family for almost a thousand years, passed down from grandmother to her eldest granddaughter; now it is yours."

"Thank you, Savta, this is very generous of you." My hand rises to clasp the pendant against my chest. Remembering the bracelet Bina gave me that morning, I pull it out of my purse and examine the row of garnets and pearls. My heart thumps at the realisation that I now have a set.

"Don't be so downcast, Kitra, there may be hope yet for Bina's recovery."

"Really? I thought Ima said that there is no known cure for this disease."

"There is a verse that says, '*the world's, and the soul's, very existence surely depends on the scent of roses*'."

"I meant to tell you, Savta, before I fell off the swing, I was just noticing how ravishing the roses smell tonight."

"The shrubs have indeed grown quite potent, though they can't possibly compare to the Damask roses my mother cultivated in my youth."

"Who wrote that beautiful line you just quoted?"

"It's from the Zohar, but its authorship is one of the world's greatest mysteries. If anyone can solve it, it's you, *querida* Kitra. You are, after all, an expert in medieval poetry," Savta Shoshanna says.

My eyelids grow heavy as I count the scintillating stars, brighter than anything I've ever seen in the city, and inhale the fragrance of the roses penetrating the room through the partly open window.

Savta Shoshanna places a gentle hand on my sore back and sings the verses of the *Song of Songs* that she sang to me as a child whenever I needed to be soothed:

I am asleep but my heart is awake, the voice of my beloved knocks.
'Open up, my sister, my beloved, my dove, my innocent one;
for dew suffuses my head, drops of the night fill my locks'.

As I slip into unconsciousness, a procession of strangers appears, claiming to be my ancestors. Though they bear some resemblance to my grandmother, I do not recognise them. One woman has my grandmother's dimpled cheek and deep-set green eyes and wears a crown on her head. Another is young and freckled and sits at a small Damascene table hunched over a stretch of silk, gracefully manipulating a needle and sliding the fabric across the table inlaid with mother-of-pearl. Yet another, wearing a satin gown, sits in a rose garden strumming a lute. The water flowing from the fountain behind her punctuates my grandmother's humming as she rocks in her chair, waiting for me to fall asleep.

Savta Shoshanna's Specialty Date Salad
Merav Fima

Ingredients:

For the salad:

    1 cup Medjool dates, pitted and halved
    1/4 cup slivered almonds
    1/2 cup fresh kumquats, peeled and halved

For the dressing:

    1 tbsp rosewater
    1 tbsp orange blossom water
    1 tbsp honey
    A dash of cinnamon

Directions:

Toss the salad ingredients together in a bowl. Mix the dressing ingredients together and pour over dates.

THE MAY 26TH CYCLE

MATT J. MCGEE

United States

According to Google, May 26th is just another uneventful, boring day on everyone's calendar. A quick check of an iPhone will show there are no major holidays on May 26th, except for something called National Paper Airplane Day. While I'm always tempted to work on my folding skills for the big celebration, I already know I'll be moving that day, just as I've moved every May 26th for the last thirty-seven years.

On May 26th, 1986, my family established our own annual holiday. And whether by design or fate, or the simple fact that our twelve-month leases always came due at the same time, we marked May 26th as the annual point when the earth would start moving beneath our feet again. For me, it's never stopped.

On the evening of May 26[th,] 1986, I was watching a Cincinnati Reds game, reclined on a stylish couch that wrapped my whole body like the welcoming hand of God himself, if God's skin were made of Naugahyde. It was only the second inning. The Reds already had seven runs on the board and two runners on base with no outs when my father walked into the den and shattered my ten-year-old's sense of perfection.

"Hey," he said. "C'mon. Family meeting."

I gestured at the TV with both arms as if to say 'Are you kiddin? Lookit this!' He switched the set off. A whine came out of my lungs. Dad pointed at the dining room.

I dragged my feet down the hall and took my usual chair. Over the next hour my sister and I listened to our mother and father announce that in three weeks, on May 26th, we'd uproot our perfectly happy lives in southern Ohio and relocate to blazing hot southern New Mexico. Years later I'd find out my parents were having a joint mid-life crisis fueled by Dad's ever-shifting sales career.

"Think of all the adventures!" he cheered.

Mom was still clearing the dinner table. The dishes were gone, left-overs stored, which made it crumb-sponging time. Mom and an army of yellow-green sponges waged a lifelong War on Crumbs: swipe with the right, collect in the left. Never dump on the floor, it only encourages the dog. Another May 26th, ten years later, after we'd landed in Boulder, Colorado, Mom took a job in a diner. She got a paycheck, a section of booths and tables to wait on, and whole snowdrifts of crumbs to wipe away.

But that first impending May 26th brought a lot of protests.

"But my *friends*," my sister Brooke said.

"You'll make plenty of new friends," Mom said. She threw the crumbs out an open window for hungry birds. Mom was an early ecologist.

"But they won't be the *same* friends."

Mom rolled her eyes. "See? Already this move is a step up."

"What's wrong with my friends?"

"Nothing." Mom sighed. "But you're twelve now, and, well, a lot of things are going to be different next year."

"Like what?"

"Never mind. You'll find out. Either way, you'll find that there's suddenly a whole lot of people you'll have outgrown."

Brooke eyed our mother. "What if you're one of them?"

"One of what?"

"One of the people I outgrow."

Our mother resumed her usual seat. "You don't outgrow your mother. You blame her for ruining your life, then make a new life for yourself. Eventually you come back and say, 'Hey Mom, look what I did despite how you screwed up my life!'"

I was confused. "Am I going to outgrow you?"

"Nope. Same answer. Either way, you'll both be shedding a lot of old friends soon, and where better to start looking for new friends than in a whole new town?"

My sister and I looked at each other and shrugged.

"See?" Dad said. "OK, now that everyone's onboard, let's talk about the new neighborhood we've picked out." He slid a brochure from a manila folder and invited everyone to gather around. I looked back at the TV, quiet and dark. The Reds were probably up ten runs by now.

The brochure was glossy, full-color, stapled like a giant copy of Life. The houses had lush green lawns and the streets seemed a mile wide. In one photo, a red-headed girl my age sprinted through an open front door, dress billowing modestly, a huge smile stretching her cheeks as if she couldn't wait to go meet the neighborhood kids. I stared deep into the picture; even then I had a weakness for redheads.

Suddenly, May 26th couldn't come fast enough.

"They're out of houses."

My sister and I traded a look of alarm like our ears and brains weren't connected. *Had we heard right? How could we drive all this way only to find the neighborhood sold out?* It wasn't like a motel that filled up or a movie theater running out of tickets. This was supposed to be the rock upon which our boat grounded ashore.

"It's alright," Dad continued. "We'll find a hotel. It'll do for a little while. Like a vacation."

"We've *been* staying in hotels," my sister pointed out.

"So the vacation gets extended."

We settled into an unimpressive one-story motel that stretched along the town's main drag. Late summer days were spent at the pool working on my tan, hoping the new school year would still bring a redhead. Maybe a whole class of redheads. Not that I was greedy, but it was New Mexico. Who knew what to expect? Just imagining it made me smile.

My sister and I passed the nights sitting on the curb, watching custom cars cruise by. Sometimes we'd wave. Some drivers waved back or honked musical horns. A few offered my sister a ride. Since saying no never seemed to satisfy a driver, she perfected the art of scrunching her nose and shaking her head.

We were reclining in a pair of lawn chairs in front of our hotel room when Dad pulled up. He loosened his tie as he approached, the tie he wore to work every Thursday. He was a traveling salesman of sorts, the difference being that we traveled with him. He held his briefcase. Mom was still unbuckling in the car.

"Big news," he announced.

My sister's brow raised. "Pancakes for dinner?"

"You wish. No. Your mother and I," he gestured at Mom, "we finally found us a home. We just put down a deposit. We move in Sunday."

"It's new," Mom said, an undercurrent of pride in her voice.

"Are there kids our age there?" I said.

"Probably." Dad shrugged. "If there are, I'm sure you'll find them."

I wanted to ask if I'd have my own room but didn't want to rock the karma boat. I was ready for our first May 26th to be over.

A third of the homes in the new neighborhood were still unfinished. There were no lawns. Streets were narrow. We were warned not to play in the bare frames still under construction, since nails and screws and various debris lay ready to puncture a kid's foot, launching an ER visit and bringing the inevitable tetanus shot.

It was too hot to bike more than a few blocks through Southern New Mexico's perpetual summer air. This limited our cultural experience to the 7-Elevens that bracketed the development. The candy tasted the same, but the kids at the farthest store near the town's largest intersection were wary of us, as if we'd just arrived from another planet. Like Ohio.

The first friend I made that year, and the only one I'd need, showed up at that exotic and distant store. Stevie was stocky like his Sinaloan father and, like me, headed to fifth grade. While I prided myself on simply having survived the move, Stevie's pride and joy was a thin wisp of mustache he was already cultivating.

One afternoon, two older girls pulled up to the 7-Eleven in a hot-running Pontiac. They slammed their doors and moved toward the neon oasis.

"Watch," Stevie said. He folded his arms, leaned against a front window and lifted his Slurpee in toast. "Ladies."

The driver rolled her eyes and didn't break her stride toward the store, out of the heat. The passenger gave Stevie a tiny smile.

"See that?" Stevie said.

"What?"

"Little smile the blonde gave me. Outta my league right now. But a few years from now? Oh yeah. It's on, baby." Stevie stroked his 'stache using his thumb and pointer, a gentle pinching motion to coax the fur along.

I started school in September with a fresh spiral notebook, binder and a few new pencils. The girls paraded into classrooms wearing their Back to School best. Stevie swiped his sister's mascara and stroked the applicator through the peach fuzz on his upper lip. He leaned back in his chair and cast a suave smile across the room.

The only girl immune to Stevie's charm was Linda. Not quite a redhead or strawberry blonde, her color was more a failed attempt at bringing a little bottle-blonde to natural brunette, as if her shorter-than-shoulder length chestnut brown was the last thing she wanted. The result was a mild Ronald McDonald orange.

Linda owned a wardrobe of once white baggy tees and oversized denim of every brand, hiding whatever figure she may have been developing. I'd later find out that everything was a hand-me-down from three older, motorcycle-crazy brothers. The random oil stains, faded handprints, and erratic chain lube marks could've become a fashion all their own.

She was perfect.

Like me, Linda didn't have a lot of friends. At least I had Stevie to commiserate with, but Linda spent lunches with her back against a storage room door in what little shade the building offered. Her arm would drape over a knee, a leather band on her left wrist. Her gaze was like a shepherd overseeing the flock, but I knew she was watching the other girls, the blonder ones, waiting to be invited into their circle.

Stevie, trying to bite into his bologna sandwich without getting crumbs stuck on his lip, noticed my stare.

"What are you looking at. That chick in the corner?"

"No."

"You like her? Man, she's weird."

"Weird? Like, how?"

"I don't know. Lives up the street from me. Doesn't talk to anybody. Why? You wanna talk to her? Go talk to her!"

I pointed at my upper lip. "You got a thing here."

"What, where! Is it gone? How about now?"

"It's gone."

"Phew. OK, I gotta hit the head. Go talk to crazy girl."

I shrugged and didn't move.

"Dude, you're gonna die a lonely old man, you don't go out and talk to girls."

"I'm too young to die an old man."

"You know what I mean. I'll be right back. Go talk to her."

Stevie bee-lined for the boys room. I imagined he'd wait until everyone had cleared out then whip out his sister's mascara. He'd stride into class, tardy, a giant grin beneath his freshly groomed stache.

Across the schoolyard Linda sat with her chin up, eyes closed, the New Mexico sun warming her skin, multiplying her freckles. Part of me didn't want to disturb her. There was plenty of time to introduce myself. We'd spend lunches together, soak up rays in a place not so lonely.

In the first week of the following May, as the Reds were playing again, my parents delivered the news: we'd be moving at the end of the month, this time to Syracuse, New York.

I never spoke to Linda, just finished my grade early and on May 26th at 9 a.m., we drove through the hot streets of suburban Albuquerque for the last time. As we passed the farthest 7-Eleven, Stevie leaned against the front window, Slurpee straw poised at his lips. At his side stood Christine Kuhn, one of our class's cuter girls. Judging by the fresh Slurpee sweating in her hand and Stevie doing his best lean into the store's tall pane window, another great summer romance was beginning.

With every May 26th after that came a new home, a new school, another set of friends who'd come and go.

1987 was a freezing cold winter in Syracuse. 1988 was a scorching hot summer in Kansas. 1989 was a pleasant time beside a river outside Scranton.

The year I left for college I had the routine down. By then I thought everyone celebrated National Moving Day and changed their addresses like clockwork. I consoled four sets of roommates, heartbroken over siblings, parents, pets left behind.

Every year followed the same pattern, no matter who I lived with. Around spring break a classmate would lead the way to a room full of kegs and coeds. A baseball game would be playing on a TV, I'd excuse myself, find a ride home and start packing.

The May 26th Cycle followed me into adulthood, creeping in right around the last week of April during the first weeks of baseball season. Maybe there'd be a visit to a TGIF with co-workers, the hostess would lead us through a bar area where a ballgame would be playing, and I'd think, the Mets are in first place? Must be the beginning of the season.

Uh-oh.

Empty liquor store boxes would be stuffed into my trunk and a roll of trash bags would be bought. I'd thin out my already thin wardrobe and begin a Goodwill donation pile in the corner.

I'd send a text to the landlord giving the obligatory thirty-day notice. No forwarding address yet, but it always works out. A trendy winter in Hollywood. A lazy summer in Gnome. A spring surfing in Hawaii followed by a summer working on an Iowa corn farm. And every May 26th, usually with a Reds game on in the background, I'd follow the siren song of transience again.

This year I ended up in a hotel for three weeks outside Los Angeles while I shopped rental ads. Hotel life wasn't so bad; I could get ice any time I wanted. I also ended up dating one of the hotel's cuter maids, Charlotte, whose shorter-than-shoulder length hair, plain white baggy tees and leather wristband felt immediately familiar.

She insisted we meet off site; she didn't want management thinking she was sleeping with guests. I realized I needed to stop doing the weekly rate thing and find a place.

I found a Roomies.com ad that listed a "Male Preferred" bedroom with private bath. I went to take a look at it with Charlotte. (It turned out to be a shared bathroom, but if I timed it just right and scooted down the hallway in a towel while everyone in the house was asleep, privacy was limitless.)

The car windows were down, sending Charlotte's brunette hair in waves as we rolled up to the address, parked and got out. She'd worn a pair of my jeans since hers were all being washed. Sitting on the porch, as a portable radio played a Dodgers game on a small plastic table was the guy I suspected had been on the other end of my back-and-forth emails.

"Steve?" I smiled.

The guy lifted a brown bottle to his lips, tilted the last of it down the hatch, let out a breath and said, "Yep."

I nodded toward Charlotte. "This beautiful lady over here is my bodyguard."

"That so." Steve's eyes roamed. "Lucky you."

Charlotte gave a perfunctory smile and wandered into the yard. Steve turned down the radio a notch. Then, with a thumb and forefinger, he pinched the thick whiskers above his upper lip. From inside my whirlwind of memories I said,

"Stevie?"

The grown version of my former classmate looked me up and down for signs of recognition.

"New Mexico," I said. "Fifth grade. Mr. Dunleavy's class.

A little smile grew under his stache. "You! You were in love with that crazy orange-haired girl."

"Linda. I think she just hadn't found the right hairdresser yet."

"She died, you know."

I froze.

"Sorry," Stevie said. "I thought you'd know by now. Leukemia. Man, that was years ago. Poor Linda."

I nodded absently. Across the yard, Charlotte was running her palm over the trunk of a mulberry. Stevie nodded her way.

"She looks like her."

"Like who?"

"Linda. Only your girl's kept her hair its natural color."

"She likes it," I said.

"Even dresses a little like her." Stevie nodded, as if recalling something important. "Christine Kuhn." He wagged a pointer finger.

"Yeah. What ever happened with her?"

His glassy brown eyes glowed. "You never forget your first love. We dated until junior high then she moved on. Can't blame her. Another summer romance. Anyway, what've you been doing? How'd you get out here from that hellhole we lived in?"

I rattled off every May 26th since New Mexico. "Now here I am. Every year, a new story to tell."

Stevie recited his own journey to the little suburb outside L.A.

"Suits me fine here, always having been a Dodgers fan." He clicked off the radio and turned toward the screen door. "C'mon, I'll show you the place."

Charlotte returned from her walk around the yard, and we followed Stevie inside.

"This here's the kitchen. One other guy's renting a room but he's rarely home, eats all his meals out so there's plenty of space in the fridge."

"OK."

"That over there's the laundry, just put your soap up on the shelf and make sure you use *just* yours."

"No problem there."

"And that there'd be your room. Bring your own furniture and so on."

I walked into the middle of the room. I inspected the ceiling, judged the slide of the window, eyeballed the modest closet space. The room, the whole house for that matter, was on the small side, the way my first room in Albuquerque had felt. But it would do. After all, it would only be for a while.

Charlotte stood in the doorway, wearing a smile I'd never get tired of. Behind her, with his shoulder leaning into the wall, there was Stevie, his convenience store window traded for home ownership, his peach fuzz fully grown out. Sunlight beamed through a hallway skylight and danced angelically upon his hair.

I said I'd take it.

Maybe, I thought, this next May 26th, I could skip a year.

Saturday Night with Pa

Farouk Gulsara

Coming of Age — Malaysia

Saturday is usually a busy day for Pa. After finishing his work at the printing press about 6 in the evening, he hurries home for his routine of fashioning up for his night out with his bosom buddies. Come what may, the appointment must be upheld at all costs, and his grooming and styling must be completed like a religious ritual. After a vigorous shower to scrub the stains of printers' ink off his skin, he inspects himself in front of a three-sided, half-length mirror, which gives the illusion of a 360-degree view of oneself.

Pa would powder himself with Himalaya on Ice talcum powder and dab his newly shaved chin with the stinging but aromatic Old Spice after-shave. Hair is next. It must be immaculate, and nothing is better than Tancho nourishing pomade. He dons a crisply ironed shirt and matching pants, creases like knife blades, and the drill is complete. This is no quick endeavour. Pa takes as long to get ready as Ma takes to tie her six-metre-long sari, as well as plaiting her long hair.

Tonight, Pa and his friends are meeting up at the newly refurbished

New World Park in Swatow Lane in downtown Penang. A businessman bought the place after the previous owner underwent a rough patch with loan sharks and lousy management. With eye-catching, Tokyo-designed, neon lights of all colours, New World Park markets itself as a place with fun and wholesome entertainment for the whole family. Of course, Pa has no intention of bringing his family here. In his world, fun and family cannot be used in a single sentence.

But today, for some unknown reason, Pa decides to take me, his sixteen-year-old son, on his Saturday outing. It must be a special day, I think, although I have no idea why. I've always wondered what Pa does when he goes out while Ma tends to our needs at home. Now I will find out.

With my limited wardrobe, which is only replenished annually during Deepavali, I am hardly spoilt for choice of dressy clothes. I sigh and choose the outfit I wore for the last festival: a grey, short-sleeved shirt with short black pants. I find moments like these awkward. I have no brothers or young male role model to consult or emulate. Pa has always been aloof, busy with work or out with his friends. Usually, I just follow the crowd. Tonight, though, I have no crowd to follow.

My choice of clothing, however, meets Pa's approval, and we set out for New World Park.

The park's sarcophagus-like entrance is paved with streams of people decked out in every latest fashion. The mouth to the city of joy is drawing in people like the slurping of jelly through a straw, like the Pied Piper leading the hypnotised children of Hamelin into an abyss of flickering lights and gyrating music. I sense this will be a night to remember.

We enter and find ourselves greeted by a confusing array of light beams hitting us in the face and ear drum-blasting pop music. There's also a lot of shouting. Young women call out to lure people to try a hand at games of chance at their booths. Throw a horseshoe onto a glass cordial bottle, aim a gun at a revolving figurine, guide ping-pong balls into bowls. Customers must know that the chance of winning is remote, but they do it anyway. Maybe they like the challenge.

We walk through the game booths and come to the brightly lit boxing-cum-wrestling rings featuring up-and-coming regional fighters with exotic names like Tara Singh, Tarzan Asia and King Kong. Pa keeps on going. I sneak a look at the snake handlers perilously mingling with their poisonous charges.

We come to the dance halls. There are three. One showcases Chinese opera, which draws attention from opium-drawing senior citizens wishing to relive mainland China's good old days. The second is where those with restless feet speed off to sweep the ronggeng girls off their feet —for a fee. But they better beware; bouncers are quite particular about post-dance flirtatious activities.

The third hall, and the evening's highlight, as far as I'm concerned, is the Big Band, a disco that belts out contemporary Western music to indulge the locals who have a newfound passion for anything Western in the wake of Malaysia's independence from British colonial rule.

I want to stop and take everything in, but Pa keeps on walking to find his friends.

"Dei, Muthu!" booms a voice suddenly behind us.

Pa turns to a trendy-looking man and flashes his nicotine-stained toothy smile. "Areh, Samy!"

Samy looks like, or at least is trying to look like, an Indian matinee star. He boasts nicely starched and creased yellow-ocher drainpipe pants, a body-fitting white shirt and carefully groomed dyed black hair and dark glasses. It is pretty apparent that he is undergoing some type of midlife crisis and is desperate to relive his lost youth. I wonder how old he really is. He gives me a friendly pat on the back. I wonder if his pat would be so friendly if he knew what was going through my mind.

"Come, come. We are all waiting for you. Today is opening night. The crowd is already building up. We got to go. Velu, Naga, Nair and the gang have already got an excellent place for us," he rattles on as he lights his next cigarette with the one he has just smoked to the butt.

Something big must be happening, I think, as I run after Pa and Samy.

We reach a theatre, which has two bodyguards dressed in Roman gladiator outfits and holding mock spears at the entrance. Multicoloured neon lights flash around the seating area, thick with smoke and the buzz of excitement.

"She used to work in Singapore," I hear somebody say. And another chimes in, "She was Miss Singapore, you know!" "I hear she has fantastic muscle power." "She has sold her soul to the devil." "She wears a charm bracelet to hypnotise people."

I wonder who on earth they are talking about. The lights dim. A stocky, bespectacled gentleman dressed in a shiny jacket appears on the stage, wearing a broad grin. Amidst the echoing PA system, he welcomes the crowd, although no one seems much interested. He goes on about the fantastic lineup of programmes arranged for the evening and promises the moon, stars and much fun, but people are still engaged in their tête-à-têtes. A musician walks on stage with his guitar and strums a chirpy song. The crowd remains unfazed. Then a juggler, a magician, an acrobatic couple and a singing duo perform their acts. Unimpressed, the public start getting restless.

The fat man in the shiny suit gallantly marches onto the stage again, still looking pleased as Punch. He is enjoying his game of playing hard to get.

"Ladies and gentlemen, the moment you have been waiting for is finally here. Specialising in modern dances, she used to dance to an uninspired crowd. One day, her brassiere snapped, and everyone started clapping. That is when she decided that a career change was due. Presenting from Bukit Bintang BB Park, the 1959 Miss Singapore, the one and only, the amazing, the adorable, the vivacious Miss Rose Chan!"

The crowd roars with thunderous claps, cat calls and wolf whistles.

The spotlights go berserk, twirling to and fro. They finally stop at the silhouette of a lady with her back facing the crowd. The spectators go wild. Music starts from a live band. I realize it's the first time I've ever heard a live band. It is nothing like the tinny sound from the neighbours' beaten-up radios. Every note and instrument sounds succinct and clear without overlap or echo.

I busy myself people-watching. Most of the crowd are boisterous old men of various races with a sprinkle of young ladies joining the merry-making. Many are drinking and smoking heavily. The smoke gives the air a beautiful aura for Ms Chan's performance. It appears as if she is in heaven amongst the clouds, and the crowd love it.

The music's decibels get louder. The beat goes faster. Suddenly, Pa pats my shoulder and says, "Parr..dah!" Look, boy! But before I can turn to see what the fuss is all about, the curtains have dropped. All I catch are flowers being strewn onto an empty stage.

I had missed the show.

Roti Canai
Farouk Gulsara

Roti Canai is a popular flatbread in Malaysia. It is usually served hot with lentil (dhal) curry.

Ingredients:

4 cups wheat flour
1 egg
3 tablespoons unsalted butter
1 tablespoon sweetened condensed milk or honey
1 ¼ cup water
1 teaspoon salt

Directions:

1. In a stand mixer bowl, add flour, salt, egg, butter, condensed milk and water. Mix well and knead for 10 minutes. Leave to rest for 10 minutes and knead for another 5 minutes.
2. Divide the dough into 10 small balls. Coat each ball generously with unsalted butter and place them in a

container that has been generously buttered. Cover the
container tightly and refrigerate overnight.

3. The following day, Spread some unsalted butter on the
    working surface. Take one ball and lightly flatten it. Press
    and push the dough with the heel of your palm to enlargen.
    Stretch the dough circle as thin as possible, until almost
    transparent. Every so often, spread some softened unsalted
    butter on it to help with the stretching.

4. Scrape and push the upper end of the dough to the middle.
    Do the same to the lower end, forming a thin, wrinkled log.
    Shape the log into a circle, tuck one end inside the other. Let
    the dough rest for 10 minutes before cooking.

5. Take one rolled circle and flatten it out. Heat some unsalted
    butter on a pan using medium heat. Place the flattened
    dough in the pan. Cook for several minutes and then flip
    and cook the other side.

6. Remove the cooked roti canai and place it on the
    countertop. While the roti is still warm, carefully grab it
    with both hands and squeeze it to the middle. This will fluff
    the roti.

7. Keep the roti canai under a cloth to keep warm. They're best
    eaten with dhal or any type of curry.

Different from All Other Nights

Rebecca Rush

Passover — United States

I'm not a great Jew. I've fasted on Yom Kippur only once, by accident, because I was on cocaine. There is one Jewish holiday, though, that I make a point of celebrating, and not just because it's fun to put weed on the seder plate where the bitter herbs go. My favorite thing about Passover is this; it's considered a mitzvah to drink four glasses of wine with dinner. It's my mother's favorite thing about Passover, too. It may be why she converted to Judaism.

I was in therapy in high school. I thought it was because I talked too much, but my therapist told me that I was really there to learn how to deal with my mother.

A lot of people have needed therapy to deal with my mother. You may need therapy to read this story about her. Toxic people don't just affect those they love, their impact spreads. When you dip your finger in your wine and drop it on your plate to symbolize a plague during seder, some hits your charoset. *Dam.*

Sophomore year, she passed out on her plate during seder. It was her fiancé's first year celebrating with us. That night was no different than any other night in that he insisted she wasn't drunk. She raised her head briefly, her face like an afikomen smushed into a dirty dish during an argument. She won.

In the morning he was gone, the dining room clean.

Junior year, they married.

Senior year, I brought a boyfriend and my two best friends to seder. Hosting overwhelms women in my family, but we do it anyway. She was drunk before school let out.

At sundown she sat across from me with one hand over her eye to stop the world from spinning. My boyfriend was straight-edge, but my friends and I smoked a blunt before we sat down. We were kicking each other as my mother's fuck-friend read, "And why is this night different from all other nights?"

My sister yelled at everyone, grabbed her plate, ran upstairs and slammed the door to watch *Buffy the Vampire Slayer*.

Steve (MMFF) continued the ceremony, "What does the wicked child ask?" My mother took the hand that wasn't over her eye and pointed at me.

After we wandered the desert for forty years, it was time to eat.

The first course is matzoh ball soup. To make the soup, you first form tiny balls from a mixture of matzoh meal, vegetable oil, and egg that has been chilled for at least twenty minutes. It helps if your hands are wet. You then drop them, one by one, into a simmering pot of chicken stock, watching them fall and puff back up as if they were your enemies. Cover and cook for half an hour. People put stock into whether your balls sink or float, but I didn't care. What does it matter when your life is a disaster?

Now I know what I like, and I make them floaters. Matzoh balls float when they're fluffy. I learned in Miami to add seltzer to the mix to be sure. Dense matzoh balls are the ones that sink, the kind they serve at famous Jewish delis like Canter's on Fairfax here in LA. Dense balls are a whole project, with a strange mouthfeel as sad as the morning after.

My mother rose to serve the first course with one hand still over her eye, like a drunken shiksa pirate.

Dina, my vegetarian friend, spoke quickly. "I can't have the soup. It's made with chicken broth, right?"

I nodded.

"Don't worry, Dina. I fixed something special for you," my mother said as she lumbered in the direction of the kitchen, the china in the cabinets shaking with her effort.

My mother was always "fixing something special for you." Once when my friend Shana (a nickname that means "pretty" in Hebrew) slept over, she went to the kitchen for a glass of water in the middle of the night and found my drunk mom microwaving leftover Chinese food. When the microwave stopped, my mother took it out and turned to her.

"I fixed something special for you!"

So, when I heard those words at seder, I shot out of my seat. I entered the kitchen just in time to see her stick her paw into the boiling pot of soup, bat out a few matzoh balls, and plop them into a Tupperware container. She opened a can of vegetable broth, dumped that on top, and stuck the whole thing in the microwave.

While it did whatever microwaves do, she served her fuck-friend and mine, spilling as she stumbled, narrowly missing the cat's head. When it dinged, she poured the contents into a bowl and staggered into the dining room proudly.

"I made this special just for you, Dina," with a flourish, like a cracked out Lumière.

Close behind, I drew my pointer finger across my neck, the classic boating signal to cut the engine. My mother had used it the year before on the front lawn, looking absolutely feral as I (grounded) rode off in a car full of boys anyway.

As the bowl moved down toward Dina, so did my own meltdown.

"Stop! There's chicken in there! There's broth! The balls were cooked in chicken broth!"

"Shhhh," my mother said as if nobody else could hear her or see me. Soup hit my toe.

"Ahm not trying to contamatize you, Dina," she slurred.

"I don't think I'm going to have the soup. Thank you, it's okay."

"I made it special for you!"

"I'm sorry. I'm not that hungry."

After we graduated high school a few months later, Dina and I went backpacking around Europe. The whole time she was obsessed with people sneaking meat into her food and would only eat at American chain restaurants. McDonald's in Paris, the Hard Rock Café in Amsterdam.

We were sitting in TGIFriday's in Barcelona when I pointed out the obvious.

"You know my mother isn't in the kitchen here, right?"

Maybe I'm a better Jew than I realize. I did just spend an entire essay complaining about my mother.

Not My Mother's Matzoh Ball Soup

Rebecca Rush

Ingredients:

Soup:

½ rotisserie chicken
32 oz chicken broth
Fresh herbs (poultry blend)
Thimble sized piece of fresh ginger & or turmeric root
6 small (not baby) carrots
3 stalks celery
½ shallot
½ sweet onion
4-6 mason jars full of water
Maldon sea salt
Fresh ground pepper
Optional: Other vegetables on hand

Matzoh balls:

Matzoh ball mix packet
2 large eggs
6 oz topo chico
2 tbsp vegetable oil

DIRECTIONS:

1. Gather ingredients, cutting board, stock pot, mixing bowl.
2. Place vegetables except for one stalk of celery and two carrots in pot along with a few sprigs of each herb (one only for rosemary, she strong).
3. Add a healthy pinch of salt and four rotations of the pepper grinder.
4. Pull most of the meat from the chicken, put it in a bowl for later (I usually leave the wing and dark meat on the bone).
5. Place ransacked carcass on top of vegetables.
6. Cover with four mason jars or so of water.
7. Turn flame to low.
8. Simmer partially covered for two hours, adding more water as necessary.
9. While this is happening, make balls according to packet directions and place in fridge.
10. Strain broth and put back in pot.
11. Roughly chop and place remaining vegetables in pot.
12. Shred and add chicken.
13. Turn heat to medium, bring to boil, then turn heat down to simmer.
14. Stay sober.
15. Don't be my mother.
16. Serve and enjoy.

The Birds Sang Tuesday

Kwasi Shade

Carnival — Trinidad and Tobago

They sang a day
when Carnival was a far-off sound
chipping over the hills
as the sun cooled, long;
jumbie chant seized the air
among fronds of confusion.
An ice cream truck was lost in Laventille.
A carousel was drowned
in marching shouts of copper reveling.
The whole of Port of Spain
was thumped with cupreous devil things.
Them trampled like mud already.
Jouvay turn people dead already.
Freedom as revenge was mas already.
Yet,
these birds clambered on a myrtle,

and sang for freedom,
same with no grit, no vengeance.
Brim was sheer possible joy;
they were sublimed by glory.

Jumbie: Ghosts, spirits
Jouvay: First day of Carnival

Trinidad Pastelles
Kwasi Shade

Pastelles are popular in Trinidad and Tobago during the Christmas to Carnival season. They consist of a cornmeal dough stuffed with meat, usually beef, and other ingredients according to preference. Some people add raisins and olives whilst others add spices to their beef or fish. They are traditionally wrapped in banana leaves before steamed in hot water.

Image by amrothman from Pixabay.

Ingredients:

Beef filling:

    2 lbs lean ground beef
    2 cloves of garlic
    3 stalks of green onion or scallions
    1 sprig of fresh thyme
    1 whole onion
    3 sprigs of fresh cilantro
    2 tbsp Worcestershire sauce
    2 pimento peppers, seeds and stems removed
    2 tbsp ketchup or tomato paste
    2 tsp black pepper

1 tbsp Knorr chicken flavor bouillon
Salt to taste
Optional:
1/2 cup raisins
3 tbsp capers
1/2 cup olives

Corn meal dough:

2 cups yellow, finely ground corn meal, such as Venezuelan
Promasa or P.A.N. (available in Hispanic grocery stores)
2 tbsp corn flour
4 tbsp butter, softened
2 1/2 cups hot water
2 tsp of salt or more to taste

Banana leaves (available in Caribbean grocery stores)

Vegetable oil, for coating leaves
Aluminum foil or string
Parchment paper

DIRECTIONS:

1. In a food processor or blender, combine the fresh herbs and pulse to form a gritty paste (green seasoning). Add the green seasoning to the beef, with the black pepper, bouillon, and salt to taste. Combine, cover and leave in the fridge to marinate several hours or preferably overnight.
2. To prepare the filling, using a heavy pot on medium heat, add about 2 tbsp of oil. Add the meat and cook until browned. Set aside to cool.
3. Next, prepare the corn meal dough. In a large bowl, combine the corn meal, corn flour, softened butter, and salt.

Gradually add some hot water and stir to form a smooth, soft dough. Cover with plastic wrap and set aside.

4. Prepare the banana leaves by gently rinsing under warm running water to make them easier to fold. Dry the leaves on both sides with paper towels and cut into roughly 8 inch squares.

5. Boil water in a steamer pot, or regular pot with a metal colander insert and cover.

6. To assemble the pastelles, a tortilla press is recommended. You can also use your hands or a rolling pin to flatten the dough.

7. Lay one piece of the banana leaf onto a flat surface, and brush with oil to coat. Form the dough into 3 inch balls and cover with a damp cloth.

8. If using a tortilla press, place one dough ball onto the greased banana leaf, then place a piece of parchment paper over the dough, and gently flatten using the press. Don't press down too hard because it might cause the dough to break when folding.

9. If using your hands, gently flatten the dough ball and spread it out evenly into a flat circle.

10. If using a rolling pin, cover the dough ball with a piece of parchment paper or plastic wrap, and gently flatten into a circle.

11. Spoon about 3 tbsp of filling into the center of the flattened dough. Fold the leaf, starting from the sides and gently massage to lift the dough from the leaf. Repeat for all sides until the dough forms a rectangular shape. Fold the leaves together like an envelope, then cover with a layer of foil or tie with a string.

12. Steam the pastelles over boiling hot water in a covered pot for about 30 minutes, then serve.

The Secret Recipe where Family is the Key Ingredient

Meredith Dylan

Christmas — United States

Like any typical family, my family gathers throughout the year for milestone events and major holidays, but we have one day that is all our own: Cookie Day.

For nearly three decades, we've picked a day close to Christmas to bake several hundred cookies, mostly to give as presents. Known simply as Cookie Day, it's become an annual tradition that has resulted in endless requests both for the cookies and the recipe, which has remained a closely guarded family secret for more than three generations. But the day's real reward has always been far more than the sweet treats, it is the treasure of spending time together. It is a reminder that despite our differences, our quirks, our busy lives, we are, above all, a family.

My grandmother started Cookie Day decades ago when my brother and I were little. Although my mom and aunt debate me on this point, I'm positive the tradition was launched at my grandparents' home in Babylon, a suburb of Long Island, New York. We later moved the operation to my parents' house when my grandmother's kitchen became too small for all the women in the family who would crowd in to help.

We use only the recipe for traditional Italian Christmas cookies that was brought from Italy by my Great-Grandma Giuseppina, whom is my mother's namesake, about 120 years ago. As far as we know, she ate them as a child in Italy with her family. The recipe has altered slightly over the years as we've had plenty of practice perfecting the concoction. My mom is sure that the addition of chocolate chips is an American touch.

Only family members are allowed to have the recipe, and they are sworn to secrecy on pain of family excommunication if they reveal it. "You will only get the recipe after you marry my son," my mother told my future sister-in-law Christy, who thought she was joking. But my mother was dead serious. Christy did not get the recipe until the Christmas after she and my brother were married. She now makes dozens of the cookies every year in her own kitchen.

Baking cookies for a large family is a lot of work. In the early days, we cranked out five batches of 125 cookies in a day, painstakingly mixing the batter by hand. Each of us took a turn stirring the heavy, sticky dough until our arm muscles burned and our backs were in agony. We first called in my dad to help us out, but eventually, we caved to modernity and bought a Kitchen Aid mixer, wondering why we never did that before.

If we thought the mixer would solve our problems, we were wrong. Our cookies got famous. People would try one and then request their own batch. Every year the number of people who wanted cookies grew. Workmates, teachers, friends, neighbors, coaches, kids' best friends' families, begged to be put on the list of recipients. Some people requested two Tupperware containers so they could hide one under the bed for themselves and the other to share with their family. My mother's neighbor offered a deal we couldn't refuse, his deviled eggs for cookies. He soon cottoned on that the more eggs he'd offer, the more cookies he'd get. Deviled eggs have now become part of our Christmas tradition.

We obliged the requests, before it simply became too much. Now we churn out about 250 cookies every December. This still requires a veritable industrial production.

On Cookie Day, we start the morning with coffee and bagels. Our core crew consists of about ten of us: my mom, her sister, my two cousins who are sisters, myself and my two daughters, and my nephew. We've also had to rope in reluctant relatives, such as my cousin's wife, who nevertheless takes her duty of doling out sprinkles seriously before speeding off to "walk the dogs."

Bags of flour and sugar, pounds of butter and chocolate morsels, dozens of eggs, and tubs of red and green sprinkles, all amassed by my mother and aunt in the days before, fill the kitchen and dining room of my parents' house. We don aprons, put on Christmas music and get to work assembly-line fashion. We all take turns as ingredient mixers, tray fillers, oven watchers, timers, sprinkle droppers, icing makers, and cleaner-uppers. Most of us are also batter eaters, icing lickers, warm cookie testers, and some of us are secret chocolate chip dumpers—my aunt Gloria and I add way more chips than the recipe calls for when no one's looking.

Before my grandmother passed away in 2021, she oversaw the process, waving a finger crooked with arthritis as she scolded and corrected. My cousin Laura, a notorious late arrival every year, has since taken on that role, telling us off if she catches us goofing off or sitting down on the job.

Our conversation follows a similar pattern every year. Aunt Gloria and my mom complain about the number of batches we did the year before and say that we won't do as many this year, while the rest of us argue that won't be enough. My mother curses my father for buying such a small oven. Aunt Gloria, who also likes to sing although not always in key, gets sick from an icing overdose.

Someone's always getting yelled at, usually my nephew Steven and my daughter Camryn, who sneak off to the living room for "unauthorized breaks," and the decorators, notably my daughter Mia, get caught tasting cookies fresh from the oven, while the rest of us have to make do with scraping bowls and licking spoons.

We inevitably talk about starting a proper cookie business. Without fail, our grandmother would chime in that she'd be the boss. No one ever argued that point, but we argue about plenty of other aspects of cookie-making and end up baking different batches according to individual tastes.

Some family members like their cookies cooked longer, while others prefer theirs doughy in the middle. Some of us favor traditional sprinkles, while others want crystal sprinkles in Christmas colors. There are always differing opinions about icing: thick or runny, more or less, none at all.

I long ago lost a campaign for blue sprinkles. My mother ruled out any color other than red, green and white, which signify both Christmas and Italy. "You can make your own at home and add all the blue sprinkles you want," she said.

We hold decorating competitions to see who sprinkles the best Italian flag. This usually results in an argument between my cousin Christine and me about who's the overall better decorator.

The only interruption to Cookie Day over the years was the pandemic. In 2020, we held Cookie Day at my cousin Laura's house without my mom, aunt and grandmother. It felt strange and incomplete. The following year, my mom and aunt made only one batch because several of us had Covid. But post-pandemic we are back on track and have more requests than ever.

No doubt about it, Cookie Day is a lot of work. We complain and roll our eyes, but I hope we never give it up because it's really a celebration of family—warm, boisterous, funny, gloriously imperfect, and mine.

FOR AMMI. EID MUBARAK

SHEERIN SHAHAB

Eid — India

The call for evening prayer resounded through the narrow, crowded lanes of the little settlement. It was much anticipated. Inside the heavily curtained houses, hungry adults offered their thanks to Allah for another day of Ramadan* successfully completed. It was the twenty-ninth day of the pious month, when Muslims all over the world abstain from eating from dawn to dusk. With the sun setting over the horizon, they prepared to break their fast.

Ammi hurried to put the iftar* on the table —a sumptuous spread of pakodas, or fritters made of onions, eggs, and eggplant, and haleem, a delectable stew made from an assortment of lentils, wheat and succulent lamb pieces, along with sparkling tall glasses of cerise-coloured sharbat rooh-afza*. However, nothing could keep Naseem in his seat on this day while the azaan* was called. As soon as the mellifluous tones rang in his ears, he ran up to the terrace, the sound of his slippers on the bare cement stairs a dead giveaway to his destination. His small stature and lanky frame at his age were a testament to the high energy levels of the eleven-year-old.

"Naseem, have a bite of the meal. There is a reward for partaking in the meal even if you don't fast. You can go to the terrace later." Ammi's admonitions fell to the ground unheard, along with the dust from Naseem's slippers.

"Let him go. He is excited about sighting the new crescent moon," Abbu said.

"You mean, he's excited about the ice cream," Ammi said.

"Anyway, if the moon comes out, today will be the last day of Ramadan. He can eat his fill later."

"Hmph! You and your ice cream." Ammi sniffed but she couldn't hide her smile. It was a family tradition. Whoever first spotted the Eid crescent that marked the thirtieth and last day of Ramadan would be treated to ice cream. It was almost always Naseem, his bright eyes sharpened with eagerness at the prospect of a delicious treat.

The two of them slowly ate the repast. After a month of fasting, they didn't need much to fill their shrunken stomachs. As they got up to offer their prayers, Naseem's excited voice came down the stairs.

"Ammi, Abbu, I found it! It is there but quite faint. Come quickly, both of you. It won't be visible for long. Come, come."

His parents hurriedly finished a few fritters and climbed the narrow stairs, prayers on their lips. Tomorrow would usher in the festival that Muslims all over the world celebrated with the greatest of fervor, Eid al-Fitr. Ammi made a mental list of all the jobs that awaited her the following day as they emerged onto the terrace.

Naseem stood on the western side of the terrace, beckoning to them with impatience. They looked to where their son pointed, straining their eyes to no avail.

"You are sure you saw it? Or you are doing it for the ice cream?" Abbu asked.

"Abbu, I swear I'm speaking the truth. Isn't the shaitan* put in prison during Ramadan? So who would make me lie then? Would he be out so soon after the month is over?" He thought a bit more and then continued with the questions. "How soon is he out, Abbu? Who is the jailer, do you know?"

The questions would have kept coming if Ammi hadn't interrupted. "There it is. I can see it. Naseem, you will get your ice cream tomorrow."

The crescent moon was little more in size than a cut sliver of lemon, largely lost in the clementine shades of sunset, but it was there. Abbu, however, still couldn't spot it. He tried running his gaze low across the horizon.

"Is this some kind of conspiracy between mother and son? Why can't I see it?"

Ammi held his finger and pointed it towards the shimmery heavenly body playing hide and seek in the waning sunlight.

"Now do you agree that you need to have your eyes checked?" she asked, a smile playing at the corner of her lips.

Naseem's father grunted and the three of them went back inside the house. As they reached the bottom stair, one of Ammi's anklets, a thin silver chain with tiny tinkling bells, snagged on Abbu's slipper and broke. Ammi picked up the pieces with sadness. It was a gift from her mother, and she always wore it.

"It had to break on the eve of Eid. I'll have no time to get another one as tomorrow will be such a busy day. Now I will have to go around on Eid without it."

The house was a flurry of activity for the rest of the evening. Ammi dispatched Abbu to the grocery store with a long list of items needed for the next day's feast. The cook had taken leave for Eid, so it was up to her to make all the delicacies. Then she cornered Naseem into helping her clean and arrange the house, which he agreed to only when she threatened him with no ice cream.

By the time Abbu returned, all the rooms had been given a makeover. Sheets had been changed, pillows fluffed, and fresh curtains hung. Ammi arranged her cut-glass bottles of itr*, exuding fragrances of rose, khus* and jasmine, on silver platters reserved for special occasions. She washed and dried her bridal dinner set of dainty bone china for the guests and pressed the new white kurta* pajama sets for Abbu and Naseem and her own fancy dress ready for Eid prayers in the morning.

Ammi started preparing food as Naseem went to bed. He was dreaming of ice cream when he was shaken awake by his mother.

"Naseem, get up. Time to go to the Eidgah* for Namaz. Hurry! Abbu is almost ready."

Naseem rubbed the sleep from his eyes and sniffed. The fragrance of sewain dipped in ghee pervaded the rooms. He licked his lips. No one made sewain* like his mother. He picked up his towel and ran to the bathroom, happily anticipating a bowl of sheer khurma* for breakfast.

When he entered the kitchen dressed in his kurta and brand-new sandals that he had chosen himself, Ammi placed a steaming bowl filled to the brim with the milky dessert before on the table. In between bites, he scratched his neck and arms. The starched cloth was making him itch.

Once he had finished, Abbu dabbed some itr on Naseem's dress and wrists. Naseem squirmed. "Keep still!" his father admonished. Naseem obeyed. The next moments were the best. Abbu hugged Naseem three times, alternating sides, as he uttered "Eid Mubarak." Blessed feast.

Joy washed over Naseem. It wasn't every day that Abbu hugged him. Most of the time Abbu was stern and gruff. But today, clutched in his father's embrace, he felt his love, and that made this the best day of the year.

"Eid Mubarak, Naseem. Come back soon!" Ammi wished him as he and Abbu left for the Eidgah. While they were gone, Ammi bathed, dressed and offered the namaz for Eid. Then she resumed cooking for the guests who were coming for the Eid feast. Abbu had invited two of his cousins with their families. It would be a large group and a lot of preparation was required.

Half an hour later, she was surprised when Naseem staggered into the house sobbing. He ran to Ammi as she came out of the kitchen to see why they had returned so soon.

"What happened, Naseem? Did someone hurt you? Did you fall down?" she said as she inspected him for bruises or ripped clothing. Everything seemed in order. She looked Naseem in the eye, waiting for his explanation. He stopped crying.

"Someone took my new sandals when we were praying." Naseem broke into fresh tears. "They were my favorite."

Ammi looked at his feet. He was wearing a pair of old slippers, almost black with dirt and worn paper thin. She smothered a smile. This happened every year at the Eidgah grounds where crowds congregated to offer Eid prayers. People would often leave their old slippers and slip away in someone's new pair, either deliberately or by mistake.

"Don't worry, Naseem. You have many nice shoes. Someone needed those sandals more than you, dear. We will buy you another pair."

Naseem sniffed. "But what will I wear today?"

"You can wear the ones from last Eid. They're still in good condition. Now go play with your friends. Don't you want to collect lots of Eidi* gifts from your friends and their parents?"

Naseem brightened, suddenly forgetting the pain of his lost shoes. "I wonder how much I will collect this year? Can I buy whatever I want with it? You never let me buy things myself," he said with a pout.

"You can buy whatever you want, even comics," Ammi said with a laugh. "Now shoo. I have work to do."

Naseem changed into his old sandals and went out with his father, skipping with joy. It wasn't everyday he went on visits with Abbu. At each stop, he gorged himself—vermicelli cooked in a variety of dishes, chicken kebabs, chhole, a spicy tangy chickpea curry, and his favorite, fritters dipped in yogurt. Before returning home Abbu took him to the ice cream parlor. It was quite crowded with excited kids, hollering their demands. Naseem got not one, but two servings of his favorite kesar pista* ice cream. He came home late in the evening, stuffed with food and clutching a handful of notes and coins.

"Ammi, look how much Eidi I collected because Abbu took me to so many places. I will collect more when I go with you to visit all your friends. I also bought something with my Eidi. Something I wanted very much."

Ammi smiled. "Yes, you will keep collecting the gifts for this whole month. Now go and wash up. Our guests will be here soon."

Naseem made a face. "I am so full. I don't want to eat anything." He patted his round tummy and burped to reinforce his point.

"Not even your Ammi's biryani?" she asked with a smile.

"Biryani? Always!" His face lit up and he made a dash for the washroom.

Three hours later, Ammi finished cleaning up after the guests. She was exhausted but suffused with the glow of a good evening spent with friends and relatives. She padded into Naseem's room to wish him good night, but he was already asleep, still in his new clothes. Wrung out from all the excitement, he hadn't even had the energy to change into his night-suit.

She pulled a cover over him and slid a pillow under his head. He had balled his hands into fists and creases from his fingers had imprinted themselves on his cheeks. She carefully unfurled his fingers. Clutched in his hands was a pair of silver anklets with a note, "For Ammi. Eid Mubarak."

Glossary

Ramadan: A holy month for Muslims in which they fast from dawn to sunset.

Iftar: The evening meal to break the fast.

Rooh-afza: A drink common in India and Pakistan, especially for iftar.

Azaan: The Islamic call to prayer.

Shaitan: Satan.

Kurta pajama: Loose fitting garments akin to a pajama set.

Itr: Oil-based perfume.

Khus: Itr from the roots of vetiver grass.

Eidgah: The designated place for offering Eid prayers.

Kesar pista: Saffron pistachio, an ice cream flavor.

Sewain: Vermicelli

Ghee: Clarified butter.

Sheer khurma: A milky dessert made from vermicelli.

Eidi: Gifts or money given to children who visit at Eid.

Haleem
Sheerin Shahab

Image by Rajib Ghosh from Pixabay

Ingredients:

For the haleem:

1 cup broken/cracked wheat
½ cup mixed lentils (1 tbsp each of chana dal or split chickpeas, masoor dal or red lentils, moong dal or split mung beans, urad dal or split back lentils)
¼ cup rice

For the meat stew:

1 kg (2.2 lbs) lamb pieces with bones (Chicken or beef can also be used.)
1½ cups oil
3 large, thinly sliced onions
3 tbsp ginger garlic paste
1 cup plain yogurt, whisked well
3 tsp garam masala or all spice powder
1 tsp turmeric powder
1 tsp chili powder

1 tsp black pepper powder
2 tsp coriander powder
1 tsp cumin powder
2 green chillies, cut lengthwise
6 cups water
¼ cup cilantro, chopped
1 tbsp mint, chopped
2 tsp ghee or clarified butter
Salt to taste

Garnish

Chopped mint, chopped cilantro, fried onion, green chillies, lemon wedges and ginger juliennes.

DIRECTIONS:

1. Soak the haleem wheat in water overnight. If using broken wheat, soak for 30 minutes.
2. Soak the lentils and rice for 30 minutes.
3. In a deep pan, heat 1 cup oil and fry the sliced onions till golden brown. Take care that they are not crowded. This will make them soft instead of crisp. Once golden, remove and put
4. In another pot, heat 1/2 cup oil. Fry the meat pieces till they turn brown.
5. Add ginger garlic paste and sauté for a couple of minutes.
6. Add the whisked yogurt and cook for 5 minutes.
7. Add half the fried onions, all powdered spices, 2 tsp of garam masala, chillies and salt. Stir for 2-3 minutes.
8. Add 2 cups of water, bring to a boil. Lower the heat, cover and simmer.
9. While the meat is simmering, put the soaked and washed wheat, rice, and lentils in another deep bottomed pot. Add 4 cups of water, bring to a boil, and then let it simmer on

low heat till the grains and lentil mixture is soft and mushy.

10. When the meat is tender and ready to fall off the bones, separate the meat from the bones.

11. Shred the meat well using a fork, hand blender or mixer and then mix it back into the meat gravy.

12. Make a smooth paste of the grains and lentil mixture using a blender.

13. Mix the meat gravy into the grain and lentil paste.

14. Add 1 tsp of garam masala, the chopped mint and cilantro, bring to a boil and then let it simmer on low heat for thirty minutes.

15. Drizzle ghee on top, add the garnish and serve hot with naan or with lemon wedges on the side.

We Are All April Fools

Cynthia Gallaher

April Fools' Day – United States

The first day of April,
the day we can lie,
to say hello when we mean goodbye.

The day to tape a quarter to the floor,
to see what fool will try to pick it up,
a day to place an apple core in sister's drawer,
or plastic bug in brother's cup.

A day when you can't wait to get to school,
and find a boy or girl to fool,
but everybody's thinking the same thing,
'cause being fooled feels like a sting,
it's salt in a wound, it's green eggs and ham,
when it's you who's lampooned, when you fall for a scam.

Is now the time to reciprocate?
Sorry, Charlie, it's too late,
to tell Jack he's got dirt on his face,
when he's just one-upped you in the April Fool's race.

But it's a long day, give the clock some ticks,
then dish out the phony compliments.
Suppose you say, "That's a lovely necklace, Annie,"
when Annie isn't wearing any.
She reaches up to touch her neck. What the heck?

All day, you need to keep on guard. You know it's hard.
Just remember if someone yells, "Your shoe's untied,"
keep on walking, put pride in your stride.
But there's a moment that makes fools of us all,
when teacher hard pitches a stunning curve ball,
and announces early when the a.m. bell rings,
"Class, listen up, no school today."
Then after we're cheering, she adds with a grin,
"April Fools! You've all got to stay."

Experiencing Judaism in the Giant of Africa

Shai Afsai

Purim — Nigeria

My host pointed to a tree-lined mountain towering on the horizon and told me he retreated there on foot to fast and meditate in seclusion.

"Only hunters and animals are on the mountain. They do not trouble me," Habakkuk Nwafor continued. "I go there to talk with God."

I was in Kubwa, Nigeria, at Nwafor's invitation to celebrate Purim, the Jewish Festival of Lots, and spend time with some of the several thousand practitioners of Judaism in Africa's most populous country. It was the first of three trips I would make in 2013–2014 to learn about Judaism there.

Upon exiting Abuja's airport terminal, I had been met by Nwafor. A waiting car took us to Kubwa, the sprawling suburb of Abuja where Nwafor and his wife, Amaka, lived with their children. For the next week, I resided with the family and accompanied Nwafor to homes, synagogues, and other sites in the area.

With no Nigerian rabbis, men like Nwafor, who began practicing Judaism in 2002, took on the task of synagogue leadership in the country. A competitive boxer in his youth, Nwafor worked in construction and raised goats and chickens, which roamed freely about his walled compound. The compound also contained Tikvat Israel, the synagogue that he directed. Bearded, lean, and muscular, he emanated religious fervor.

Nwafor and Tikvat Israel's congregants were Igbo, members of the country's third-largest ethnic group, who considered themselves to be descendants of Israelites they believed arrived centuries ago in what is now Nigeria.

Most Igbo, whose traditional homeland, Igboland, is in the country's southeast, are Christian, but many Igbo, even while practicing Christianity, nonetheless regard themselves as genealogically Jewish. The phenomenon of Igbo identification with Jews dates at least to the 18th century when they encountered Christian missionaries. The Igbo noted similarities in the missionaries' Bible between their customs and those of the ancient Israelites. Influential Igbo, such as the 18th-century writer Olaudah Equiano, concluded "that the one people had sprung from the other." This is an opinion shared by many Igbo today. It concretized during and after the Nigerian civil war (1967–1970), in which at least one million Igbo died in the failed bid for Biafran independence. In the past few decades, several thousand Igbo, including the worshipers at Tikvat Israel, have taken this genealogical self-identification a step further and embraced rabbinic Judaism as their lost heritage.

The day after my arrival in Kubwa, dozens of people began flocking to Nwafor's compound to see me. It was the dry season, with noon temperatures exceeding 100 degrees Fahrenheit. A mighty cashew tree that once shaded his courtyard had fallen in a violent storm a few years earlier, so we sought shelter from the sun in a palm-frond hut next to the synagogue.

Among the visitors were four prayer leaders and Hebrew teachers who traveled over eight hours by bus from Igboland to meet with me. The knowledge and proficiency of these four men, three of whom were in their twenties, was remarkable, especially as they had managed to learn much of Jewish tradition through the internet.

Late into the night, they chanted Hebrew prayers and played religious songs they had downloaded to their cellphones. The power often went out in Kubwa, especially in the evening, and residents relied a great deal on flashlights and generators. We sat in Nwafor's courtyard, the thick darkness illuminated only by the blue glow of their cellphones, the air filled with music and talk of Judaism in Nigeria, the United States, and Israel.

The oldest of the four visitors, a musician named Chislon Eben Cohen, was among the first Igbo Jews to master Hebrew, which he did in part by obtaining materials through the mail from the Academy of the Hebrew Language in Israel. He then imparted his knowledge to others in the community.

"When I see adults and elders struggling to learn alongside the younger ones, I find encouragement for my efforts and know I must work harder," he told me.

Hearing this, Nwafor urged him to continue teaching despite the health challenges Cohen was facing. "We must make sacrifices if we are to establish ourselves," Nwafor stated in his distinctly raspy voice.

To thrive in Nigeria, Igbo Jews must be sturdier and more resilient than Nwafor's felled cashew tree. Yet despite their relative isolation from Jews in other countries, the people I met were practicing a joyous, forward-looking Judaism, composing their own prayer melodies, and learning Hebrew.

During my second stay in Kubwa, Nwafor reserved a time for us to climb Byazhin Mountain, the place where he went to fast and meditate and where Tikvat Israel's congregants now sometimes held prayer services. It was no longer a site only for hunters and animals. On a Friday morning, we set out in a group of eight men and ascended to the Jewish prayer location at the summit. A church group also sometimes used the summit for prayer in a small building it had constructed. The Jewish prayer area was demarcated by stones. The Igbo Jews and their Christian neighbors appeared to peacefully share the mountaintop.

While they lack centralized leadership and are not clustered in a geographic area, Igbo Jews in certain ways recall the San Nicandro Jews of southeast Italy or the Abayudaya of eastern Uganda. The San Nicandro community converted to Judaism and mostly immigrated to Israel in the 1940s. In recent decades, the Abayudaya converted to Judaism through special Conservative and Orthodox rabbinic courts set up in Uganda.

There are significant differences, though. In part due to the Igbo Jews' scattered locations, lack of centralized leadership, and greater numbers, neither mass immigration nor collective rabbinic conversion is likely to occur soon. Self-identifying Jewish groups that do not have documented historical connections with more established Jewish communities face considerable challenges in gaining rabbinic recognition, particularly as genealogical Jews.

Still, given their growth and tenacity so far, I believe Igbo Jews will continue to solidify their identity. More Jews abroad will become aware of, and take an interest in, the development of Judaism in Nigeria. Several books, a full-length documentary, dozens of scholarly articles, and numerous op-eds and newspaper pieces (frequently churned out by writers who have never been to the country) have focused on Nigerian Judaism.

In my case, I was not only welcomed and hosted by Igbo Jews during my three stays, but Nigerian government officials and media people also offered to assist me as I continued to learn about Judaism in the country. Other travelers and locals have not always fared as well. In 2021, for example, three men who came to Nigeria to film part of a documentary about lost tribes of Israel were arrested and imprisoned, along with a local Igbo Jewish woman who was helping them.

My first stay in Nigeria was timed to include the celebration of Purim, which commemorates the deliverance of Jews in the Persian Empire from the villain Haman and his followers, who had planned to annihilate them, with King Ahasuerus's initial acquiescence. In the end the tables were turned, Haman was executed, and — after King Ahasuerus decreed that Jews be permitted to defend themselves — his supporters were defeated in battle. The heroes of the Book of Esther, the cousins Mordecai and Queen Esther, established a new holiday, Purim, to commemorate the Jewish victory:

Mordecai recorded these events. And he sent dispatches to all the Jews throughout the provinces of King Ahasuerus, near and far, charging them to observe the fourteenth and fifteenth days of Adar, every year — the same days on which the Jews enjoyed relief from their foes and the same month which had been transformed for them from one of grief and mourning to one of festive joy. They were to observe them as days of feasting and merrymaking, and as an occasion for sending gifts to one another and presents to the poor. (Esther 9:20–22)

A focal point of the Purim holiday is the public reading of the Book of Esther from a Hebrew scroll, and the Book of Esther was chanted at Tikvat Israel on the night of Purim, as well as on the following morning. Having a festive meal that includes drinking alcohol, especially wine — one reason being that several crucial turns in the Purim narrative involved consuming wine at royal banquets — are also traditional ways of observing the holiday. This was done in Kubwa too.

While costumes are popular in other countries, neither Igbo Jewish children nor adults wore costumes in Kubwa. Nor did anyone there eat *hamantaschen*, the triangle-shaped pastries most associated with Purim today, or any other holiday-specific foods.

But as is customary elsewhere, noise-making of various kinds took place during the public readings of the Book of Esther. I had brought with me special Purim noisemakers, called *ra'ashanim* in Hebrew, and passed them out to some of the children. Whenever the name of the villain Haman was mentioned during the readings, the children shook the noisemakers to drown it out.

Prior to the holiday, Nwafor had prepared an effigy of Haman, whom King Ahasuerus ordered hanged from the same gallows the villain had constructed with the intent of killing Mordecai. Late at night, several of the men and I hung Haman's effigy from a noose erected near the synagogue so that it would be on display in the morning.

———

Holidays such as Purim unite Jews across the globe. The Igbo Jews' small numbers — perhaps 3,000 in a multi-ethnic country of over 220 million people, the Giant of Africa — did not concern them, since they viewed themselves as part of the wider Jewish world. But there was no doubt that their remoteness from other Jews complicated matters of study and observance.

"We are adherents of the Jewish faith in Nigeria. We are neither Christian nor Muslim," Pinchas Azuka Ogbukaa, one of the friends I made in Kubwa, told me as we sat in the shade of Nwafor's palm-frond hut. He was referencing the country's two dominant and state-supported religious groups. "Belonging to neither of those faiths is not even the problem. The greatest of all the challenges we are facing is that of isolation. Bridges of Jewish education and worship have to be built, connecting us with other communities in the United States and Israel."

Several months later, Ogbukaa traveled to Rhode Island to see me and meet my Jewish community. It was the first time he had left Nigeria. He timed his stay with Sukkot, the Festival of Booths, giving us another chance to celebrate a Biblical holiday together and share our religious heritage.

When I eventually put together a photo-text exhibit based on my time with Igbo Jews, people in Nigeria insisted on contributing funds to help cover part of the costs involved in informing people in Rhode Island about Judaism in the country. The photo-text exhibit opened in 2014 at Providence's Brown RISD Hillel, the center of Jewish life at Brown University and the Rhode Island School of Design. Some of my favorite photographs in it were of the Purim celebration in Kubwa.

Hamantaschen
Shai Afsai

The name of these traditional Purim cookies is thought to refer to Haman, the villain in the Purim story, or to poppy seeds. This recipe by my aunt, Chava Miedzinski, a vegan cook, has no grain or nuts, and no added salt, oil, or sugar.

INGREDIENTS:

1/4 cup flax seed
1/4 cup tiger nut flour
1 tbsp tiger nut flour
1/4 cup coconut flour
1/2 cup unsweetened fruit preserves
Optional: a pinch of ground cinnamon, ginger, cloves, allspice or cardamom

DIRECTIONS:

1. On a small plate, mix 1 tbsp of tiger nut flour and a pinch of your preferred sweet spice and set it aside.

2. Grind the flaxseed and 1/4 cup of the tiger nut flour together.
3. Mix the dry ingredients in a bowl.
4. If you are using fruit preserves or jam with chunks, strain it and transfer the larger pieces from the strainer to a separate cup to use for the filling. If you are using jelly, you will not need to strain. (You can also use frozen blueberries or chopped nuts.)
5. Mix 1/4 cup of the strained fruit preserves into the dry ingredients in the bowl. Mix very well into a dough and knead it into a big ball.
6. Roll the ball into a log shape and break the log into 4 to 8 pieces depending on how big you want the hamantaschen. These will not be very big.
7. Shape each piece of the dough into a ball.
8. Press the ball flat on the plate with the spiced tiger nut flour. This will keep the dough from sticking to your hand and will add taste to the hamantaschen.
9. Form a triangle shape by pressing 3 sides upward to form a well in the middle.
10. Fill the well with the chunks from the strained preserves (or other filling).
11. Pinch the corners of the triangle to close the sides as much as possible over the fruit filled well. Repeat with the rest of the dough.
12. Place the triangles on a cookie sheet, covered with parchment paper.
13. Bake at 350 degrees for 25 minutes.
14. Allow the hamantaschen to cool completely on the sheet before transferring them, or the cookies might break apart. They will harden as they cool.

Makes about 8 small or 5 bigger hamantaschen.

THE AMIGO DEAD

JOHN GREY

Day of the Dead — Mexico

Shop windows are adorned
with papier-mâché skeletons,
some in cowboy hats, some with crowns,
Behind glass, slumped together,
they look like drunkards at the end
of a party.

Soon enough,
they'll join the parade
with catrinas bearing flowers
and blasting, bellowing,
mariachi bands.
Their showy heads,
ritualized out of all horror,
will jiggle on springs
as their loose limbs scuttle and prance.

These are dead
assembled for joy and liberation.
They're the dead you can cheer
from the sidewalk
as they dance to the song of life.

These aren't the dead
who confront you,
face to skull,
and demand you join them.
They're the friendly dead,
the amigo dead.

Lick a sugar skeleton,
cake with white frosting
like twisted bones.
It's the Day of the Dead,
a lively celebration.

RITUALS OF LIFE
EVIE GROCH

Bar Mitzvah — Israel

On a warm Friday afternoon, their car slowed as they came out of the light curve in the road. A family strolled toward them, taking up the breadth of the street with no apparent concern for traffic. The young mother had on her head scarf and long skirt, holding the hands of her two small daughters, was resolute, head held high and eyes judging the car's occupants. Her husband, clad in a black suit, black hat, and sporting side locks, walked beside her, holding hands with their two slightly older sons. The car braked to a standstill.

Hannah and her husband Carl heard her Israeli cousin, Dov, who was driving them into Jerusalem, muttering under his breath. They couldn't go forward without running the ultra-orthodox family over, and the family wasn't getting out of the way.

Still mumbling, Dov put the car in reverse and backed out of the street. Carl and Hannah held their breath. They were on their way to the downtown Jerusalem hotel, the closest one Hannah's daughter could find to the Western Wall, the location of their grandson Adin's Bar Mitzvah that was to take place the following week. The entire family had come from Northern California for the ceremony and to reunite with Hannah's extended family in Israel.

Organizing the ceremony had proven a challenge due to the restrictive rules of orthodox Judaism, which dictates that men and women must pray on separate sides at the Wall. The Torah isn't even allowed on the women's side, but sometimes, in the spirit of celebration and with the help of a man who supports women's rights, it would be handed over the barrier to the joy of the receiving women. But that could result in a demand for its return, and a stalemate would ensue. It was a controversy Hannah's daughter wanted to avoid. Still, Adin's Bar Mitzvah would involve both men and women reading from the Torah. They couldn't hold the ceremony in a place where one sex wasn't allowed.

Luckily, an excavation had recently uncovered an extension of the Wall at its southern end, and the new area wasn't governed by the orthodox rabbinate. It would be the ideal spot to have family members of both sexes read from the Torah and the rabbi bestow the title of Bar Mitzvah on Adin. He had been practicing his Hebrew and writing his speech for months.

Hannah and Carl had left Zichron Yakov in Northern Israel early enough that morning to arrive in Jerusalem before sunset and the start of Shabbat, when everything would close, including their hotel. Now their plans had literally run into a road bump.

Dov found an alternate route, but it, too, was filled with ultra-orthodox families coming out of their homes to stroll in the streets and deliberately block traffic. Dov backed out again, his muttering becoming louder and his hands gripping the steering wheel with determined force, as though strength alone could contain his growing anger.

After they encountered the same scene on several streets, Hannah and Carl feared Dov was about to explode in a rage and do something drastic. Hannah suggested they roll down the window and explain to the people they just wanted to pass through their neighborhood.

Dov laughed. "Are you crazy? You really think that would do any good? Don't even bother."

"Why not?" asked Carl.

"Because they are deaf to you. They won't answer."

"Why are they doing this?" Hannah asked.

"Because they can. The police won't get involved."

"No, I mean, why are they doing this right now?"

"Because Shabbat is coming soon, and driving on Shabbat is forbidden."

"But it's not Shabbat yet," Hannah said.

"I know that, Hannah. Everyone in the country knows it, but there's no arguing with them. The ultra-orthodox own the streets in this part of the city, and the government won't step in. It's a losing fight."

"So, what do we do? The hotel will only hold our reservation until sunset."

"I'll keep trying to find a way around them, but I am losing patience."

Carl and Hannah sat quietly, having no other suggestions and not wanting to further upset Dov. As they prayed for a way out, they watched other cars being attacked. Fists pounded on their hoods, yells rang through the air. A few punches were even thrown. What a way to welcome the Sabbath, Hannah thought, far worse than driving.

Dov tried one more time to turn into a street that would lead them out of the neighborhood, but again found it blocked.

"Damn," he shouted. "I'm going through them! They'll get out of the way soon enough!"

"No!" Hannah and Carl yelled in unison. "Stop!"

"I don't want to be part of this," Hannah said. "Let us out. We'll find a way to walk through."

"Okay, okay," Dov said. "But I give up. I don't know what to do."

Carl, who always had good spatial awareness, suggested Dov try a new maneuver.

"We've been intuitively making right turns, trying to head to Jerusalem, which is just south of us. Why don't we turn left, make a wide circle, and go east or west to find another way out of this area?"

"Okay, I'll try."

In about fifteen minutes, they were on a clear road leading to their hotel. Hannah and Carl breathed a sigh of relief, but they were still shaken. Hannah's mind flashed back to a few years earlier when she and her sister had visited Israel. They were touring the famous city in the hills, Safed in the Northern District. It was one of the most picturesque cities Hannah had ever seen, and located at an elevation of 3,000 feet, it was the highest city in Israel. Its mystical quality encouraged the study of Kabbalah, and scholars flocked to it. The mild climate was also a welcome respite from the humid lower elevations in the summer, and the views were spectacular.

As they walked along the narrow streets, Hannah's arms covered by three-quarter sleeves and her sister's with a light shawl, a group of young Hasids approached. The women prepared to nod to them as they would anyone else, but the men made a barrier with their hands to block their view of the unfamiliar women. Hannah knew that the ultra-orthodox were not free to have contact with women other than their wives and family members, but still, she found the gesture insulting. Hannah's sister laughed, taking it all in stride. She deemed them foolish and fanatics. Hannah, though, didn't find it funny. It was as if the Hasids were trying to deny her very existence as a woman. Just because they don't see us doesn't mean we don't exist. Now this, with ultra-orthodox families blocking the route to their hotel. She wondered if there was anywhere in Israel that they didn't exert influence or make others feel excluded.

Once she and Carl were settled in the downtown hotel, they found it included a bountiful breakfast buffet that Israelis do so well. Almost every culture was represented in the array of foods. However, on Saturday morning, the extensive daily spread was replaced by a single table with cheese slices, bread, fruit, cereal, hardboiled eggs, and juices.

When they asked about the breakfast, they learned that in order to respect the rites of the ultra-orthodox since they made up the majority of their guests, food prepared using electricity—stoves, ovens, toasters, waffle makers, espresso machines—wasn't served on the Sabbath. The elevators had even been set to "Shabbat" mode where the car stopped automatically on every floor since pressing a button was considered work, which was not permitted on Shabbat.

In the evenings, Hannah and Carl would take taxis to go to dinner with their relatives. Most of the drivers were Arabs, who knew the best ways to get around Jerusalem. They shared with one their experience trying to get into the city that fateful Friday afternoon. He laughed.

"You should come in my taxi. I know how to stay out of that area. I have a special way to go. Next Friday, if you want to go out, take my card and call me. I will take you wherever you want to go, and we will be free to go anywhere."

They took his card, just in case.

Every night after dinner, Hannah's relatives gathered in the huge lobby where they talked for hours over drinks and hot chocolate for the kids, met newborns and new in-laws, and exchanged family news and gossip. Carl and Hannah usually sat against a wall with a good view of the other side of the lobby. On the first night, Carl told Hannah what he had observed on that side. Intrigued, Hannah decided to pay attention the following night.

As Carl had described, two sets of parents, one accompanying their daughter, and the other ushering in their son, were led in by a matronly, scarfed woman, who introduced everyone and seated them on a spacious sofa. Then she and the parents left.

The young woman was conservatively dressed in a light-colored, long-sleeved blouse tucked into an ankle-length dark skirt. She had long dark hair and translucent skin that made her appear angelic. She watched her parents walk off then shifted her gaze to the young man at the other end of the sofa and offered him a demure smile. He was swarthy, dressed in a black suit. He removed a wide-brimmed black hat to reveal a black kippah (skull cap). His beard was short and well kept. His black shoes were so highly polished, Hannah was sure he could see the lights hanging from the ceiling in them. The couple were clearly engaged in small talk, but Hannah was too far away to make out the language.

Hannah looked at Carl who smiled and nodded at her, as if to say, "See, I told you." Soon they saw other couples being led in the same way. Some young men and women seemed to be meeting for a second or third time. Hannah realized it was matchmaking, and the woman who ushered in the families had to be a *shadkhn*, matchmaker. At least, they got to meet each other before the wedding, Hannah thought.

Every night thereafter, Hannah and Carl made a point of arriving early in the lobby to get a good seat for the show of this courting ritual. Some of the young women wore lace hair coverings, but their hair flowed freely from under them. Once they married, their hair would only be shown to their husbands in private. Some might even go so far as to shave their heads and wear a wig. One night they spotted a young woman wearing makeup, which was unusual. She was attractive enough to resemble a model. The men would often order a beverage for the two of them, usually coffee or tea, perhaps with a cookie or two. Hannah would have loved to hear what their conversations were about. She wondered how educated the young woman was, if she would be able to continue her education after marriage and children.

The rest of the family caught on to what Hannah and Carl were doing and started observing, too, making sure to keep an unobtrusive distance. They started laying odds on which couples they thought would make it to the altar and which wouldn't. Hannah and Carl took a special interest in the first couple they had seen. After three nights of watching them sit feet apart on a long sofa, they sadly gave them a thumbs down on making it. But on the fourth night, the couple moved closer together, and by the fifth night, they were almost touching. On the other hand, several of the couples Hannah and Carl had given a thumbs up disappeared after a few nights, although perhaps they simply decided to meet elsewhere. But Hannah and Carl soon got better at reading body language and predicted most of the couples correctly.

The day of the Bar Mitzvah arrived. Adin performed admirably and his parents made praising speeches in his honor. At the age of thirteen, he was now considered a man. As the ceremony drew to a close, a line of other families with their rabbis and Bar Mitzvah boys waited for their reservation time at the southern end of the Western Wall. Good thing they had been first, Hannah thought.

On their last night in the hotel, Hannah decided to ask the barista who had been making her mochas along with small talk, about the matchmaking ritual they had been observing. He was happy to fill in the missing pieces. This hotel was a safe place to meet in public. These couples would not be meeting in bars or at parties. If they got to a dinner date, the hotel dining room would serve them a kosher meal. They could stay overnight in separate rooms.

"What if one doesn't like the other?"

"No problem," the barista said. "Either of them can call it off. It's not like old times when only the parents got to decide."

How liberal and civilized, Hannah thought. She held back from asking her final question: Does the *shadkhn* get paid only after the match is sealed?

As Hannah and Carl left the hotel the next morning, full after their breakfast feast, Hannah kept replaying the lovely courting scenes in her head. All the couples were intriguing, nice looking, trusting, respectful, and devoted to their beliefs. Would she ever have the occasion to meet them, befriend them, or would she simply run into them as they blocked the street with their children on the way to Jerusalem?

Sweet Lokshen Kugel
Evie Groch

Ingredients:

1 cup raisins
12 oz wide or extra-wide egg noodles
6 large eggs
2 cups sour cream
1 cup cottage cheese
1 cup (8 oz) cream cheese, softened
1 cup sugar
1/4 cup unsalted butter, melted
1/4 tsp salt
Cinnamon and sugar combined for dusting
Nonstick cooking oil spray

Directions:

1. Preheat to 350 degrees F. Cover the raisins with hot water and let them soak to plump while you prepare the other ingredients.
2. Bring a large pot of water to a boil. Add the noodles to the pot, bring back to a boil, and let them cook till tender (not

overly soft), about 5 minutes. Drain and return the cooked noodles to the pot.

3. In a food processor or blender, mix together the eggs, sour cream, cottage cheese, cream cheese, sugar, melted butter, and salt.

4. Pour the egg mixture over the cooked noodles in the pot and stir till well combined.

5. Drain the raisins and pat dry. Stir them into the noodles.

6. Spray a 9x13 inch baking dish with nonstick cooking oil. Pour the noodle mixture into the dish.

7. Top the kugel by sprinkling generously with sugar and cinnamon mixture.

8. On a rack in the middle of your oven bake the kugel for about 60 minutes, turning once halfway through cooking, till the center of the kugel is set and the tips of the noodles turn golden brown. Remove from the oven.

9. Let the kugel rest for 15-20 minutes before slicing. Serve warm or cold. Makes 10-15 servings.

A Lifelong Passion for Estonian Jaanipäev

Kaja Weeks

Midsummer — United States

I grew up far from Estonia, a little country facing the Baltic Sea that was my parents' homeland. Yet celebrations from those roots were sown within me from birth. As a child, I was especially enchanted by Midsummer, *Jaanipäev*, and it became a lifelong fascination. This tradition, which celebrates the longest days of the year and the glory of sunlight, takes place June 23 and 24 with the night in between when dusk is said to kiss dawn.

We would travel from the suburbs of northern New Jersey to an Estonian community space in a pine forest at the other end of the state. Many Estonian customs were kept alive there, including the magnificent bonfire of *Jaaniöö*, Midsummer's Eve.

I was just a slip of a girl when I first became riveted by the bright tongues of flame soaring into the darkening sky, the pops of blazing wood and sparks dancing in the air. The deeper meaning of the celebration was not yet clear to me, but I knew that it was connected to ways of beauty and yearning for my family's homeland, which they had left in the wake of World War II.

At that time, with refugees freshly arrived, well over a hundred people would show up. Generations mingled, from infants to grandparents, and most everyone knew each other.

The evening was preceded by an afternoon of camaraderie around traditional foods, drinks, and most importantly, indulging in long saunas. Saunas have been part of *Jaanipäev* for centuries. Indeed, they form part of daily life in Estonia where they are used for relaxing and socializing, especially during the long, dark winters. Estonians sit naked or wrapped in a towel in the hot steam with good company, using birch branches with their leaves for an invigorating massage. I will always carry within me the unique sound and fragrance of branches whisking the skin. Stints in the heat are alternated with cold showers or dips in an adjacent lake, or even sitting in a cozy room with cold drinks and snacks.

Early on Midsummer's Eve, big logs were dragged from the surrounding woods to a central site for the much-anticipated evening bonfire. Kids were encouraged to gather plenty of dry branches, brush or paper scraps for kindling. Then a sturdy foundation and top logs to fuel a long-lasting fire was built. I loved watching the artful construction and first spark of fire as the crowd chanted *Sütti, sütti*—Light up, light up—until yellow and red flames blazed high and the scent of wood smoke filled the air.

We sang Estonian songs around the fire until well past midnight. The words were filled with lilting vowels laced like pearls between flickering consonants—*Jaan läeb Jaanitulele, kaasike*—John goes to the St. John's Day bonfire, *kaasike*. (June 24th is the birth of St. John the Baptist.) The verses painted pictures of a young man and his silk-tasseled, silver-beaded horse pulling a brass carriage with gold coins glinting in its wheels. Next to Jaan (John) sat a rosy-cheeked maid, his beloved.

Elders told stories of how *Jaaniöö* was the time of the midnight sun, which faded slowly until vanishing for a short while before returning to light the new day. The long days left no room for night, only a dreamy twilight. They whispered about the *sõnajala õis*, a blossoming fern in the forest that would bring luck to those who found it, especially young couples in search of love spells. It would be some years until I grasped that the midnight forays to find the glowing plant could only be a myth since ferns don't blossom. But the luminous, woodland image stayed in my child's eye, reappearing decades later as poetic metaphor in my writing.

Sometimes, as the fire grew lower, a brave soul would leap over it. This ritual was one of many rooted in pre-Christian times and was meant to bring good luck. In the pagan era when *Jaanipäev* was known by other names such as *Pööripäev*, Turning Day, which reinforced the significance of seasonal change, countless customs with other-worldly connotations prevailed. Once the Christian calendar came into effect, the day melded with the nativity of St. John the Baptist, and the appellation of *Jaan* (John) took hold, hence the English translation of *Jaanipäev* as St. John's Day even though the celebrations in Estonia do not hold any religious value. Rather, ancient meanings of the day marking the end of spring sowing and forthcoming summer haymaking held strong, with rituals to ensure prosperity for the remainder of the year.

At *Jaanipäev* spirits were asked to bestow luck on livestock and crops. There was a strong belief that the light of the Midsummer fire would protect against evil, night creatures, one of the reasons everyone was urged to partake. Particularly before the 19th century, vocalized charms and spells along with many fascinating magical rituals were common. Historical accounts give examples such as bathing in morning dew, which was believed to bring beauty, health and luck. People kneeled in the grass and brought dew to their faces with moistened hands. Or, in the evening they took a cloth, such as a shawl, to the meadow and pulled it through the grass until thoroughly wet. Then the precious dew could be squeezed into a bowl or even preserved in a bottle.

Such hints of nature's primal power still color the holiday. Even if participants no longer believe in the ancient magic, some rituals, such as leaping over the fire, still pay tribute to the power of spirits and nature.

Had I been born and raised in Estonia, I might have reveled endlessly in *Jaaniöö*'s airy allure. But like many things anchored in history, particularly those passed through family kaleidoscopes of loss and ensuing trauma, darker colors among the summery green were eventually revealed. My parents and 80,000 others had fled their homeland after two successive invasions, by the Soviets and Nazis, and in advance of a third, the Soviets again, that would brutally subjugate their compatriots. They longed and grieved and raged. Their will to preserve their endangered culture permeated their lives and their children's so that even celebration and beauty carried undertones of mourning and resolve.

My contemporaries in Estonia certainly were heaped with hardship behind an iron curtain for nearly fifty years. Life was grim with massive deportations to Siberia, censorship, and oppression of individual free will. Certain songs, writings and holidays, including Christmas, were forbidden and had to be celebrated in secret.

The Midsummer holiday, miraculously, escaped prohibition. I hoped that for home-Estonians, as we called them, this was one day where young and old could escape to a joyous, bewitching time. I believe our kin drew profound power from the land itself. Estonia has always been infused with polytheistic reverberations in which trees, rivers, and other manifestations of the natural world are alive with spiritual meaning.

Midsummer is a spectacular time of the year in Estonia, an interlude of white nights and the peak of flowering beauty, fields where spikes of golden rye rise among blue cornflowers and scarlet poppies, woods, roadsides and meadows filled with myriad wildflowers. On the heels of the solstice, Midsummer is a call to harness nature's brightest time.

Across the ocean, the Estonian diaspora's celebrations are contained in half a night and maybe part of a day then we return to unremarkable towns and cities, distant from each other and filled with workaday English. But in Estonia, by June 23rd, cities and towns empty as most people vacate their daily dwellings to seek nature.

As through the ages, they gather birch branches for saunas and to decorate indoors and out, including horses and farm animals, and wildflowers to braid into wreaths for girls' hair. They prepare *Jaanipäev* feasts with lots of dairy foods since early summer's rich grass yields the best cows' milk and brew a special fermented alcoholic drink, *Mõdu*, made with water, birch juice, honey, local berries, fruits and spices.

Our bonfires in South Jersey's Pine Barrens are wonderful, but their effect is subdued in comparison to fires throughout an entire land—on hillsides, farmyards, forest edges, riverbanks, and beaches. On the islands, old boats are transformed into festive pyres. Village swings also become a center of play and singing. These swings are giant wood structures on which two to eight people stand on opposite planks, grip upright beams and rhythmically rock toward the sky.

We didn't have those incredible swings in New Jersey, but with fire crackling in the background we heard stories about them from our parents and grandparents, who also taught us the "swinging songs." I was smitten by the old dialects and tunes. *Veli hella vellekene, tee meil kiiku kiitusmail.* Sweet little brother, make us a swing on the green. *Kiigu, kiigu kõrgele.* Swing, swing high.

These lyric expressions proved a critical influence in my life. They explain how a girl—who experienced an esoteric celebration in a rare language from a faraway place upon whose shores her foot had never stepped—embarked a life-long path to make Midsummer her own.

I became a professional musician, and I loved the traditional music of Estonia so much that I performed it, studied it and visited a free Estonia to hear more of it. Lyrics filled with descriptive metaphors linked to nature moved me and led me to study scholarly books and archives that documented history and held extensive field recordings. Some of the narratives that most appealed to me had themes of *Jaanipäev.*

The recollections of songstress Minna Kokk were especially gorgeous as she described how everyone, young and old, was expected at the bonfire. "Dozens of fires at dusk that shone like stars in the sky, so many you couldn't count them," she said. She described dancing, swinging on the big wooden swing, and the romantic search for a magical fern blossom with an "evening kiss, that on *Jaanipäev's* next morning still burned on a maiden's lips."

I listened to song recordings in folkloric collections made by musicologists in the early 20th century. One woman, named Marie Sepp, was from Kolga-Jaani parish, a relatively isolated rural area in southern Estonia. She was seventy-four years old in 1937, when her *Jaanipäev* songs were recorded. "Come to *Jaaniku* (the St. John's bonfire)," she sang. "Come tend the fire, be on guard for the sparks." I was overjoyed to learn the catchy melody and found it moving to sing along to a woman who had been born around the same time as my great-grandmothers.

Perhaps the most astonishing revelation through my research came through reading the book *Hõbevalge* (Silver White) by Lennart Meri, the first president of Estonia after the country regained its independence in 1991. He was also a renowned writer and anthropological filmmaker whose reconstructions of history included scrutinizing indigenous poetry. These runic verses were passed orally from generation to generation and a phenomenal collection is preserved in the country's archives.

Meri suggested that the *Jaanipäev* bonfires may have been spurred by the Kaali meteorite, which fell upon an Estonian island, Saaremaa, around 4,000 years ago. A cataclysm with an impact comparable to the Hiroshima blast, the meteorite fell upon a lightly populated area and was widely witnessed in the skies of the Baltic Sea region. I understood Meri's suggestion that *Jaanipäev* traditions may be re-enactments from the ancient fireball's earth-shattering incident when I read archaic verses memorializing the event. "I saw Saaremaa burning," is among the descriptions in songs, reflecting a belief that the sun had fallen to earth. In one of my visits, I stood on the island at the meteor crater site, which survives as a small, round lake, rock-rimmed and full of dark water. Enveloped by June's light, I was mesmerized. Time seemed to stand still as ancient connections stirred within me.

Decades later, I published a collection of my poems inspired by my ancestral roots. A composer from California, Brigitte Doss-Johnson, came across it and was so inspired by one of the poems, *Midsummer Birches*, that she set it to choral music and created a virtual chamber choir to perform it.

The piece contained my English language poem set to Doss-Johnson's composition, which was also woven with a traditional *Jaanipäev* song in Estonian. To my astonishment, singers from Estonia, the United States, Canada, Japan, Spain's Basque region, Malaysia, and Australia learned the lyrics in Estonian, one of the world's most difficult languages. Choristers sang the calls to come to the *Jaaniöö* bonfire with claps, shouts and stamping feet and four-part a cappella voicework. The result was a portrayal of Estonian Midsummer through a vibrant and mystical sound palette. The performance, in the form of a music video, was released globally online on June 24th, *Jaanipäev*.

I had not only come full circle with my lifelong passion that started when I was a little girl, but I had also done my part to ensure that the rich culture of my ancestral homeland reached the wider world.

Estonian Egg Butter (*Munavõi*)

Kaja Weeks

Inspired by the rich grass growing season, this is a perfect dairy spread for *Jaanipäev*, the Estonian Midsummer celebration.

Ingredients:

3 hard-boiled eggs
4 tablespoons (1/2 stick) of softened sweet butter
1 tablespoons chives, finely chopped
1 tablespoon dill, finely chopped
1 teaspoon mustard of choice
Salt and pepper to taste

Directions:

1. Boil eggs for 10 minutes, then plunge into ice water.
2. Peel when cooled. Use fork to mash yolks to creamy consistency.
3. Chop egg whites fine or chunky, as preferred.
4. Combine eggs with all other ingredients.
5. Use a small wooden spoon to lightly whip to airy consistency.

6. Spread generously on squares of black rye bread (*leib*) or optionally on thinly sliced cucumbers.

A Feast to Remember
Perin Marolia

Parsi New Year — India

When the wheels of the plane landed with a bup, bup, bup, at Mumbai airport, my heart went jump, jump, jump. It had been a long flight from New Jersey, but I was instantly alert with excitement for the upcoming Parsi New Year celebration that we had come around the world for.

Mom, Dad, and I moved to New Jersey seven years ago when I was four. I don't recall much about my early life in Mumbai, but I do remember how all four grandparents fussed over me. My memories came true to life when they met us at the airport full of hugs and smiles.

As we sped into the city in their airconditioned cars, I was disappointed not to see a single cow on the road, nor any snake charmers. Wasn't India full of them? I asked Dad.

"None in the cities, Roshni," he said.

Then, we were home, that is, the home of my dad's parents, who I called Bappa and Bappi, short for Bapawaji (paternal grandfather) and Bapaiji (paternal grandmother). My mother's parents I called the common Indian names for grandfather and grandmother, Nana and Nani, instead of the Parsi words Mamawaji and Mamaiji. Over the main door hung a fat string of yellow and orange marigolds intertwined with red roses.

"That's called a *tohrun*," Mom told me. "We put it over the door on all special occasions."

I was still gawking at it when Bappi sprinkled rice over our heads to welcome us. Waiting inside were my aunt Persis and uncle Cyrus and my cousins Myra and Freya, who live two floors above. I lost count of the hugs and kisses.

The rest of the day, the grownups said, was for resting. Not for me, though. I spent the afternoon and evening with my cousins who were on their midterm break from school. We watched Netflix and played board games and paper and pencil games. Finally, sleep caught up with me. I had to be shaken awake for dinner.

There was a long to-do list for the next few days, including sightseeing, shopping, and picnics. But I was waiting impatiently for the Big Day, New Year.

"It's going to be a foodie day, Roshni," my cousins warned me, "We Parsis are great foodies."

Parsis are a Zoroastrian community of Persian descent who settled in India in medieval times to escape persecution for our religion. We have our own distinct calendar, and this year our New Year's Day fell on the 16th of August.

The morning after our arrival, Dad asked what was on the agenda.

"First things first," Mom said, raising an index finger. "Shopping."

My aunt's chauffeur drove Myra, Freya, Aunt Persis, Mom and me to the Palladium shopping centre. I was amazed at how grand the place was. It could've been at home in New York.

Mom issued my instructions. "Roshni, get yourself a dainty thing to wear to the fire temple on New Year's Day, something formal for dinner that night, and something light to wear during the day, and you can pick up jeans and stuff to wear back home."

We hopped from one designer outlet to the next. I picked up twice as many outfits as I was meant to, but Mom said it was okay, the prices were fine. Then came a sea of jeans under a "Sale" sign. I filled my shopping basket to the brim, meaning to filter out the best before I got to the cash counter. Mom looked at the price tags and to my surprise, approved the whole lot with a wave of her hand. "Take them all. We've got a bargain."

Mom had picked up a lot of outfits herself. "We should have brought a suitcase. It would be better than carrying all these separate packages," she grumbled.

Aunt Persis gave a twinkly grin. "I suspected this would happen. That's okay. I put an empty suitcase in the back of the car." She pulled out her phone, called the driver. A few minutes later, he appeared with the suitcase. Aunt Persis was apparently an old hand at looking after foreign guests.

"Today we'll go sightseeing around the city. Some great architecture to take in," Bappa announced at breakfast the next day. My cousins and I made faces like sleepy frogs.

"You'll change your mind very fast, kids," Bappa said with a laugh. "But first, Sam," he said to my dad, "there's something that we do at this time every year. Bring your smartphone."

He and my parents trooped into his study. I followed them curiously. Bappa picked up a small pile of papers from his antique desk and handed it to Dad. "These are the appeals for donations that I have received. They are all deserving. I shall be sending some money to all of them. You can choose the ones you would like to donate to."

Mom and Dad leafed through the papers.

"A girls' school asking for donations in aid of orphans and poor children? It's the first time I have heard of it," Mom said as she read one of the appeals.

"They have some boarders from families in the villages. They are so poor that they can't afford to go home for the holidays," Bappa said.

I felt a strange tightening in my heart. Here I was, spending an awesome holiday far from home, having loads of fun with many family members around, and there were girls spending New Year at school. I could feel myself tearing up.

"Bappa, how much would it cost to give these girls a grand party on New Year's Day?" I said.

He thought for a minute and named a figure that amounted to about two weeks of my allowance.

"Please Dad," I grabbed his arm. "Please send the amount to these kids for them to have a party and take it out of my allowance."

"Sure," Dad said softly. "How kind of you." He tapped out the fund transfer on his cell phone.

Bappa gave me a big hug. "That's the spirit of Parsi New Year, Roshni."

Soon afterwards, Aunt Persis packed Mom, Myra, Freya and me into her car for the sightseeing tour. The three of us wiped off our froggy expressions and tried to look enthusiastic, or at least polite. But once we started sailing along Marine Drive, with the sea and the salty breeze to the right and elegant buildings to the left, I was hooked, fascinated by the sights.

Aunt Persis wove through the streets of the main business area, pointing out the landmarks. "That's Vidhan Bhavan, the building where the ministers of the government have their meetings." The upper part of the building looked like an upside-down pudding with a fluted exterior, but uniquely graceful. "That's the Rajabai Tower in the university campus." The clock tower was adorned with complex, ornate, antique carvings, as were the other buildings on the campus. We moved on slowly. "Next to the university is the High Court." Another building with splendid, elaborate architecture.

"Oh, this traffic," Aunt Persis grumbled as we waited at a red signal.

The signal turned green, and we cruised along till we got to another busy junction.

"Look to your left now, Roshni, another impressive building, the headquarters of the Municipal Corporation, After I turn right, go on watching to the left. That's an important railway station."

I gaped at the intricate beauty of the architecture. "All these buildings look so similar. How do you tell them apart?"

The scenery soon changed to old, plain buildings, some in need of a coat of paint. A little further on, Aunt Persis called out, "Look to the right. That's a big public library." The grand building bore a slight resemblance to Hogwarts. "And behind that," she continued, "is Myra and Freya's school."

"Does your school also look like Hogwarts?" I asked cheekily.

Myra nudged Freya and winked. "Yup, and we play quidditch too." They burst into giggles.

"Now look to the left. That's Flora Fountain." It was simply beautiful, a white structure with carved figures on its four sides topped with a statue of a woman. Water flowed from various points. Next the massive Gateway of India, which was shaped like a huge portal. Standing by the sea, it was built to commemorate the visit of King George V, the first British monarch to visit India in 1911.

"And now we are at the Taj Mahal Hotel." Auntie turned in through the gate and handed the car over for valet parking. We proceeded to the coffee shop to hog.

Day three dawned rather cloudy, and it soon showered. But that did not put us off. Mom wanted to meet her cousin who lived in a suburb called Bandra. So, we set out in a different direction from the previous day.

She pointed to a bridge that looked like a cousin of the Golden Gate Bridge. "That's the sea-link. It'll get us to Bandra very fast."

That's when I remembered something important. "Mom, we haven't bought any shoes."

"No problem. There are shoe shops galore in Bandra."

She was right. I did well there.

At last, the Big Day arrived. I woke at seven and wandered into the kitchen, where Bappi was giving instructions to the cook.

"Good morning, Roshni, and Happy New Year to you." She enveloped me in a hug. "Get ready soon. It's going to be a busy day."

I rushed to bathe and put on one of the pretty dresses I had bought at the mall. Soon everyone was in the hall, wishing each other *Saal Moobaaruck*, Happy New Year.

The celebrations started with breakfast — *akuri*, eggs scrambled with onions, tomatoes, and a bit of this and that. Mom makes it at home, but this was five-star. To add to it, there was *sev*, made of super thin vermicelli with a layer of nuts and dry fruits on top and eaten with sweet yogurt.

"No second helpings, please. You have to save your appetite for lunch," Bappi declared.

Then came the gifting ceremony. I watched drop-jawed as the maid decorated a space on the living-room floor. Using shallow boxes perforated with designs and filled with powdered chalk, she sat down, tapping the boxes so the chalk fell on the floor in the shapes of roses, horse shoes, fish, and other designs to form a decorative border. On top of the designs, she added colored powder from tubes. The rectangular area on the floor looked as glamorous as a Persian carpet.

"Step into the decoration, Roshni," Bappi said.

I stepped into the blank space in the middle of the design and stood demurely as she placed a dot of red liquid on my forehead. She then pressed rice on the dot and sprinkled grains around my head. All the family members came up to me one by one with hugs and gifts. My cousins went through the same ritual, and we distributed the presents we had brought from the United States

"Hurry up and get yourselves into the cars," Bappa said. "We're off to the fire temple." As we left, I noticed chalk designs at the entrance to the house, and a thick *tohrun* above the door.

The fire temple was decorated similarly, but on a much larger scale with a huge chalk design and an enormous aromatic *tohrun*. We had just stepped through the gate into the large front corridor, when someone tapped Bappi on the shoulder. It turned out to be family friends, and there were hugs and *Saal Moobaarucks* all around.

From then till we reached the temple's main room, we bumped into at least a dozen other family friends. Inside the temple, a fire burned in an urn in a room that only the priests could enter. We placed sandalwood in a tray for the priest to put in the fire. Then we folded our hands and prayed.

Next came lunch back at home. It started with a famous Parsi dish, fish coated in green chutney and steamed in banana leaves. Then came boiled rice topped with yellow lentil gravy, mutton in a sweet and spicy gravy topped with potato straws, and chicken cutlets. For dessert there was an assortment of sweets, including one made of solidified sweetened milk and set in a fish shaped mould. Everything super yum. I was so stuffed, it was an effort to get off my chair.

Afterwards, the adults snoozed while we cousins chatted, played games, and exchanged jokes until we were summoned for tea.

We found the dining table loaded once again with goodies—cupcakes, crunchy savories, Parsi cookies, and chocolate biscuits, to be washed down with tea for the adults and mango milkshakes for the young ones.

Dinner was at a restaurant at a five-star hotel, where they offered a menu of Parsi fare. We started with *Saal Moobaaruck* toasts, clinking glasses of whisky or wine for the adults, juices for us kids. For starters, there were golden fried prawns, mutton kebabs, and skewers with chicken liver and roast potatoes. The main course was the Parsi signature dish, *dhaan shaak*, an aromatic spicy lentil dish with bite-sized pieces of tender lamb served with brown rice.

There was more — *faarchaa*, chicken legs wrapped in spiced semolina, coated with egg, and fried, plus sheep brain cooked in spiced onions and tomatoes, and fish slices coated with red spice and fried to a crisp.

"I am stuffed. I shan't have any dessert," Mom said. But when she saw the decadent chocolate goodies the others had ordered, she changed her mind.

Days later, I was still so full I had to practically roll myself onto the plane for the flight home. Parsi New Year in India surpassed my expectations. It was indeed a feast to remember.

Steamed Fish in Green Chutney
Perin Marolia

Ingredients:

Traditionally, pomfret is used; but any firm white fish like tilapia can be used.

6 cloves garlic, peeled and chopped
2 teaspoons cumin seeds
2 green chillies. Split them lengthwise, remove the seeds and chop.
1/2 cup fresh grated coconut, or desiccated coconut to which a little water is added.
1 cup coriander (cilantro) leaves
2 teaspoons sugar

Salt to taste
1 teaspoon lemon juice

Traditionally, the fish is wrapped in banana leaves and steamed, but greaseproof paper or aluminum foil can be used.

DIRECTIONS:

1. Put the garlic, cumin seeds and chillies in a blender, and blend until fine.
2. Add the grated/desiccated coconut and continue to blend.
3. When smooth, add coriander, sugar, salt, lemon juice and blend. Set aside.
4. Cut the fish into pieces, approximately 3 inches x 3 inches.
5. Coat them with the chutney.
6. Brush the center of the banana leaves/foil lightly with oil.
7. Place the fish on them and wrap; tie with thread if required.
8. Steam the fish for 10 minutes.

THE REAL MEANING OF HYGGE

JASMINE TRITTEN

Christmas — Denmark

Hygge. There is no direct English translation of *hygge*. It's a Danish concept for a feeling of cozy warmth, contentment, and wellbeing. It's become a fashionable word in English in recent years, a lifestyle to aspire to. But for me, *hygge* is about my childhood, especially wintertime and its highlight, Christmas.

I grew up in a villa called Seaside, on the Danish side of Oresund, the strait of water that separates Denmark from Sweden. Winter brought short days and long nights, and deep, freezing cold. But it also brought plenty of *hygge*.

As the season set in, my father often took my two younger brothers and me for rides on Blue Bird, his iceboat, which had thin blades to skate on the ice and sails to catch the wind. Bundled up in coats, we'd put on our skates and hang on to the back of the boat as it glided over the frozen water at high speed, our cheeks turning ruddy with cold.

When snow was thick on the ground, *Far* took us to *Dyrehaven,* a large forest park with hundreds of deer, on a horse-drawn sleigh. He'd wear a gray felt hat with a pheasant feather stuck in the band. My brothers and I would snuggle under the heavy wool blanket as bells attached to the horse's harness jingled with its every step making a melodic tune. I loved to watch the horse's breath dissipate into the crystal-clear air like smoke from a chimney. After our outings in the cold, we always warmed up at home with eggnog or hot chocolate.

The best part of the season was Christmas, of course. We would decorate a crisp, green fir with a shimmering white star on top, real candles in gray lead holders, red and white braided hearts, snowflakes, and angels. We swirled a garland of Danish flags, a white cross on a red background, around its circumference. Around the house we'd put *julenisser*, Christmas elves sewn by my mother, who wore round, dark brown glasses that matched the color of her short, curly hair. Excitement built as presents wrapped in paper of all colors of the rainbow appeared under the tree, ready to be opened on the night of December 24th.

Our family gathered around five o'clock, which would already be dark on Christmas Eve. White candles were lit on the tree, in the windows and on an advent wreath, which had red ribbons woven through it, that hung from the ceiling. We always had a metal bucket filled with water next to the tree in case of fire, which happened, especially with the wreath. It would fall to the floor in flames, but my father poured water on it right away.

Glogg, a warm, spiced mulled wine, was served for the grown-ups and non-alcoholic eggnog for the kids. Dinner was usually served around 6 p.m., followed by walking around the tree while singing Christmas hymns and songs. Finally, we'd open presents and sometimes go to midnight mass at the Lutheran church.

One year proved unforgettable for my eight-year-old self. It was an especially chilly day. Large snowflakes had fallen steadily forming a white blanket over the landscape. My brothers and I kept looking through the windowpane, waiting for *Julemanden,* Santa Claus. We wondered if we had been good enough this past year to receive any gifts, and if his reindeer would make it through the snow. Tall white candles illuminated every window of the house. Flames from the smaller lights on the Christmas tree flickered, causing dancing shadows on the walls of the living room. Heat radiated from the fireplace as the aroma of my mother's ginger cookies permeated the air.

As we were about to sit down for Christmas dinner, the doorbell rang. Everybody jumped up from their seats and ran into the hallway. Carefully, *Far* opened the massive oak door. There was *Julemanden* in all his red-suited glory with a large burlap sack slung over his shoulder bulging with presents. Our eyes widened. Grinning, we jumped up and down with anticipation. *Far* invited him to take a break from the heavy snow in the warmth of our home, and following custom, he took out a few *kroner* from his wallet to give to Santa for charity.

Santa reached out his arms to greet us children. I seized his hand. It only took a moment to recognize that soft, silkiness.

"It's *Farmor!* I can tell by her hand. I know because she has the softest hands in the world," I shouted. "It's Grandma!"

As I hugged and kissed her, tears rolled down my cheeks and *Farmor* pulled off her long, white, woolly beard and wig. "I knew it was you," I said. I was so proud I had uncovered her trick.

My dad shook his head in disbelief. How had he not recognized his own mother? Both my brothers looked stunned and completely confused. They were only four and six years old at the time and still believed in *Julemanden*. How could Grandma be Santa? What about the real Santa? My parents told them that Grandma liked pretending to be Santa, but the real *Julemanden* would check on them when they were asleep.

Nobody knew my grandmother's astounding plan except for *Mor,* my mother, who had gotten suspicious when she could not find her earlier that evening.

After we calmed down, we dug into our traditional Christmas dinner of roast goose stuffed with apples and prunes, red cabbage, and small, golden-glazed potatoes. Then we had *Risalamande,* a rice pudding with a whole almond hidden in it. Whoever found the nut in their portion would receive a present. Everybody gobbled it down until my youngest brother Carsten bit into the treasure. He received a huge bar of chocolate with marzipan and refused to share it with anybody.

Following dinner, we all walked around the tree singing Christmas carols until the candles burned down. I was tired but it was finally time to open our gifts. A beautiful doll with blonde curls in a pinkish dress for me and toy cars for my brothers, who were still wondering about Santa. For the rest of the evening, we played with our toys, and stayed up until late snacking on oranges, apples, mixed nuts, and my mother's Christmas cookies.

To me, that is the real meaning of *hygge*.

RISALAMANDE
Jasmine Tritten

A delicious traditional Danish Christmas dessert made of rice pudding mixed with whipped cream, sugar, vanilla, and chopped almonds. Served on Christmas Eve chilled and drizzled with warm cherry sauce.

Photo by Rasmus Gundorff Sæderup on Unsplash

INGREDIENTS:

½ cup short grain rice
4 cups of whole milk
Seed from one whole vanilla bean or 3 tablespoons vanilla sugar or extract
3 tablespoons white sugar
1 cup blanched finely chopped almonds (Except for one whole almond to hide in the pudding)
2 ¼ cups whipping cream, whipped
Sweet cherry sauce

DIRECTIONS:

1. Bring milk to a boil in a large pot.
2. Add rice and simmer until tender while stirring often. (About 40-50 minutes)

3. When rice has thickened, remove from heat and cool.
4. Add sugar, vanilla, and chopped almonds.
5. Fold in the whipped cream.
6. Chill in refrigerator for 1-2 hours.
7. Serve with warm cherry sauce on top.

Getting Drenched in History at Armenia's Water Festival

A. Shydian

Vardavar – United States

As a child, I knew I had Armenian ancestry because my great-grandmother was Armenian. She carried many old traditions with her. I remember waking up at my grandparents' house and going the kitchen for freshly baked cinnamon rolls and *ghapama*, a pumpkin stuffed with everything and anything. For breakfast she would stuff it with fruit, rice, and nuts, making it a rice pudding with the sweetness coming from the pumpkin.

Most of the traditions she carried on were related to food, at least the ones I can remember. I asked my mother if she remembered any others. My mom remembered her singing songs in Armenian to her grandchildren when they were young. But since I grew up hours away from my great-grandmother in a mostly mainstream American home in Central Oregon, my Armenian roots seemed distant and anchored well in the past.

It wasn't until I had my own child decades later that I wanted to learn more about my heritage. I started studying Armenian culture and history and places where I could connect with my roots.

Outside Armenia, only a few locations have large Armenian populations, Chicago and Glendale, California, are the best known in the United States. But in my research, I found smaller, less well-known Armenian enclaves, including one in Oregon's Willamette Valley, a 150-mile-long region that runs south from Portland to Eugene.

Every year, the Armenian community in Portland continues a tradition thousands of years old, Vardavar, a harvest festival where everyone gets doused with water in good fun. I was intrigued, and I knew I had to go.

Vardavar was originally a pagan holiday to honor Astghik, the goddess of water, beauty, love, and fertility, but through the centuries it has transitioned into a holiday bridging the old beliefs with Christianity. It is not to be confused with Vardavar in Iran, which is the name of several villages and towns. The festival's name in Armenian means "rose burning" (*vard* is rose and *var* is burn) because offerings of roses would be burned to honor Astghik so she would bless crops and provide water and nourishment to sustain families in the upcoming year.

Despite the spread of Christianity and the Armenian Apostolic Church, the engrained tradition persevered but took on a different meaning. The rose no longer symbolized Astghik, but signified the transfiguration of Christ, the miracle that bestowed rays of radiant glory upon Jesus on a mountain. It also added the sprinkling of water on festivalgoers. Many in Armenia claim this was added because Noah commanded his descendants to shower water on each other to remember the great flood.

The Vardavar is always held 98 days after Easter, which allows for the remembrance of Jesus as well as the connection to the historical festival honoring Astghik. But now instead of bringing roses to burn and traditional foods to eat, you need to bring a towel and a change of clothes.

My first Vardavar, I sat at a distance and watched children and young adults run around a city park with buckets of water that they threw on each other. Everyone got drenched. I wasn't keen to get wet. I noticed that while some people came to the festival with a cooler full of water balloons, others used buckets that they filled from the park's water fountain. Being my first water festival, I stayed on the sidelines. I didn't know if there were any unspoken rules surrounding it, plus I felt like a fish out of water, pun intended. I saw that while it was mostly younger individuals, sometimes parents and even grandparents were pulled into the circle. Coming in as a stranger, all by myself, no one looked at me oddly, but no one went out of their way to pull me into the circle where most of the water activities were taking place. I mostly wandered around, speaking with vendors and food trucks while listening to the Armenian music.

The next year I decided to attend again, mostly because the people were so friendly, and made me feel at home, even though I don't carry an Armenian name. This time, I sat closer to the action. I wasn't sure I wanted to participate just yet. I still felt like a stranger, as if the festival didn't really belong to me.

At first I only ate the Armenian foods served at the event, but as the day wore on and the sun grew hotter, the water looked increasingly inviting. I walked down to the main group throwing water at each other and stood on the outside of the circle. Before I knew it, splashes came my way, and I was thoroughly wet. Suddenly, I was in the thick of things, laughing as I not very successfully tried to run away from more splashes.

I noted the joy in everyone's faces. Whether they were getting drenched, eating, or just relaxing listening to the music, everyone seemed happy. Generations of families sat together, watching the younger family members run around throwing water and laughing at the carefree antics. In fact, without knowing what was going on, an observer could consider the festival a very large, boisterous family gathering in the park.

Vardavar is not a serious celebration, nor overly ceremonial. There was a brief introduction at the beginning of the day from a community leader, thanking us for attending and wishing us a blessed year, then it was pure fun. A live band played music and food was everywhere. Food trucks, caterers, and potluck-style meals at large family tables, where everyone was welcome to tuck in. There were also a lot of plant vendors. Most of the plants, I noticed, were not simply decorative. They produced fruit and vegetables, intended to be planted and maintained.

After attending Vardavar, I felt closer to my great-grandmother in a way that I hadn't felt since she passed away. I was moved at being surrounded by others sharing my same ancestry and touched to be accepted by them, even though I don't speak the language and no longer use my Armenian last name. I started to visit an Armenian caterer in the Portland area, and experience different traditional foods. I found a couple of other Armenian festivals or gatherings that I plan on attending in the future. Above all, I felt my great-grandmother watching me learn about our culture and history, and smiling.

Armenian Rice Pilaf
A. Shydian

Pilaf is a staple of Armenian cuisine that can be made with either rice or wheat as the base. It can serve an entire meal, be it breakfast, lunch, or dinner. It is usually made in a large batch to keep for multiple meals. It is occasionally topped with walnuts, pine nuts, red beans, cabbage, mushrooms, and while not as common, ground meat.

My grandmother Agnes would make the recipe as a whole meal, using a traditional method of using just the base ingredients. When my mother made it, it was always the first dish gone on the table. My pilaf skills aren't up to their level, but my daughter's pilaf rivals that of my mom's (but don't tell her that).

This recipe can be easily scaled for large gatherings. It tastes as good if not better reheated. I admit I have eaten it cold, and it still tasted great.

Ingredients:

6 tablespoons butter
1/2 cup vermicelli or other thin noodle
1 cup long-grain rice
2 cups hot chicken broth (or water)
Salt to taste
Pepper to taste

Directions:

1. Melt butter in pan on medium to medium high heat.
2. Add noodles and sauté. You may need to break the noodles in half to fit, but don't break them any smaller.
3. Gently stir until noodles are evenly brown. If butter starts burning, turn down heat.
4. Add rice to mixture and stir to coat the rice in the melted butter.
5. Once mixed, pour in chicken broth or water.
6. Bring to a boil.
7. Turn down heat to allow mixture to simmer.
8. Cover and simmer for 15 minutes or until liquid has been mostly absorbed and the rice is soft. Don't lift the lid unless you have to because it will affect the rice's cooking.
9. Remove from heat and keep covered for 10 minutes. Do not remove the lid.
10. After 10 minutes remove lid and gently stir with wooden spoon.
11. Can be served on a platter or in the pan.
12. Season with salt and pepper to taste. Makes 4 servings.

The Feast of the Virgin

Anita Haas

Feast of the Assumption — Spain

"Try it on, Soli. You're so saintly, it'll look perfect on you."

Soli looked at her cousin with misgivings, then at the blue and white cloak with longing. "We'll get in trouble."

"They're all over at your house. They won't be back for ages," Pati argued, lighting a cigarette.

"No, Pati, the cigarette. My mother will kill us."

"I don't care. My mother lets me smoke. God, it's hard to believe they're sisters!"

Soli lifted the cloak to her chest and turned to the mirror. "It seems kind of ... sacrilegious to put it on. It's the Virgin's cloak."

Pati rolled her eyes. "Don't tell me you still believe in that crap?"

"What crap?"

"All that hocus pocus they made us learn in school. All those stories about saints." She took another drag from her cigarette.

"I don't know. I always liked the stories about saints."

"All that suffering. Hair shirts and self-flagellation. I mean, why would anyone want to whip himself?"

Soli hugged the garment to her body. "Haven't you ever felt that you were really bad and that maybe by suffering, by doing penance, you could be ... cleansed ... of your sins." Her voice trailed off. She had never put these feelings into words before.

Pati scoffed. "So, a good beating will cleanse you? What does sin mean anyway? What do any of us have to repent for? What have you ever done that was bad?"

Soli cringed, but Pati, busy admiring her own reflection in the mirror, didn't notice. She ironed her chestnut brown hair now, and wore bangs cut straight across. Her eyes were heavily made up and today she wore white knee socks with her green sequined mini-dress.

Since General Franco's death the winter before, Pati and the other girls at school hiked up their skirts, wore make-up, smoked, and listened to British and American pop music.

Pati even had a boyfriend, although she didn't pay much attention to him. And they talked about politics all the time, especially Pati and her older brother Fernando, and their parents. Soli wasn't able to follow, let alone participate in any of the heated political discussions and debates about the future of Spain as new democracy.

People also talked a lot about freedom and travelling to other countries and learning English, which had been looked down upon during the long dictatorship. Young people were experimenting with sex, alcohol, drugs. Soli found it unsettling, frightening even. She drew back from it all and spent more time with her grandmother and younger cousins, who also felt out of sync with the changes overtaking Spanish society.

Fernando would be the first in the family to attend university and Pati was excited about her own future in a big city. "I can't wait to get out of this hick-town, too," she said. She took another deep drag on her cigarette and threw her head back to exhale a jet of smoke. Lately she was always imitating Faye Dunaway, that is when she wasn't imitating Jane Fonda. "Fernan had better be ready, 'cause I'm going to stay with him in Madrid every weekend." She tossed her cigarette butt on the floor and stomped on it.

She looked her cousin up and down, then shook her head. "Why do you wear that crap?"

Soli was wearing a home-made brown skirt that hung crookedly, a cast-off white blouse her mother was given in one of the houses she cleaned, and a green sweater that *Abuela* had grown too wide for. Her lifeless black hair was tied in a long ponytail.

"You should rebel. Dress more modern. I certainly wouldn't take the shit you put up with from your mother." Then Pati broke the sour-turning mood. "Come on. Try on the cloak." She took the cape, hand-embroidered by their mothers and grandmother for statue of the Virgin to wear during the Feast of the Assumption in August and draped it over Soli's shoulders. "Now, with pride. Raise your head and throw your shoulders back."

"The crown. Where is it?" Soli said.

"*Abuela* was polishing it this morning. Over there, on the bench." Pati ran to get it and placed it on her cousin's head.

They both gasped at the transformation. All Soli's frumpiness instantly disappeared. Pati was right; she looked like the Virgin Mary herself. Soli admired herself dreamily. She swayed from side to side, enjoying the soft rustle of the fabric as she imagined herself a princess, a queen even.

"Soledad!"

Soli froze in mid swirl, the cape flapping against her, and cowered as her mother raced through the kitchen door and showered blows on her head. Dressed in her usual black mourning, she was like an angry, flapping, squawking crow. "Tramp! Soiling the Virgin's clothes!" She yanked the cape and crown off her daughter and slapped her face for good measure.

"Oh, come on, Dolores. They were just having fun. Don't beat her for that."

Dolores turned to face her heavily pregnant sister standing in the doorway. "You can spoil your children as much as you like, Esperanza," she shot a look at Pati in the corner "but don't tell me how to raise mine."

Espe shook her head. *Abuela* and little Manu, another of Espe's five children, entered.

Manu turned to Soli. "I saw him."

"Saw who?"

"The bad man. In the castle."

"Don't listen to him, Soli." Pati pulled him away. "He's been talking about that for a week now. Just making up stories. Anyway, you have nothing to worry about, Manu. The bad man only punished girls." Pati chortled, but Soli never thought the story was funny.

Legend had it that long ago a man who lived in the castle kidnapped bad girls and locked them up in the tower where he would subject them to all sorts of torture as punishment. The worst that could happen to bad boys was receiving a piece of coal from the three kings on Christmas. When Soli was little, her mother always threatened to send her to the "bad man."

"No, they are not stories," Dolores said from the table where she was folding the rescued cape. "Don Ramón, a rich man from Madrid, has bought the castle from the old count, and is going to restore it."

Abuela snorted. "Rich and crazy, I'd say. Anyone who has the money to buy and restore that old place has the money to live in style in the city."

Not long ago, Pati and Soli would climb up the hill, dive under the castle's broken fences, and enter the overgrown grounds. Soli used to ascend the crumbling steps of the towers and imagine herself a princess. Young lovers snuck up there to be alone, and sometimes gypsies or vagrants camped out there.

Manu tried to reclaim their attention, "You should see it. The whole property has a strong, new fence around it. But I got through."

Dolores interrupted him again. "The new owner has hired me as his housekeeper."

This was happy news. Dolores and *Abuela* took in washing, but not many people in town could afford to send out their laundry. Sometimes Dolores cleaned houses for ladies in town, but she never lasted long. There was always some confusion as to who the boss was.

"And Soli too," Dolores said.

Soli gasped.

"You are sixteen now and can learn to work. God knows you aren't much good at school, or anything else."

Esperanza spoke up. "Really, Dolores. You might let her at least finish the school year, be with kids her age. She's all alone, poor thing."

Soli flinched. She knew her mother would take that badly. Dolores had no sons, and her husband was estranged. For her, it was as if Esperanza had called her half a woman.

"I can't afford to have a lazy daughter loafing around the house. If you want her, you can have her. Otherwise, I'll send her to her father in Germany once and for all," Dolores said.

Shipping Soli off to her father had been Dolores's other constant threat during her childhood. As a little girl, Soli used to imagine her father a heroic knight like El Cid. She told herself he was in Germany making a fortune and would come home one day and buy them a big friendly house, like Esperanza's, and Mother would finally smile. But as she got older, Soli discovered the truth. Her father had returned to Spain long ago and was living in Madrid. And he was no El Cid.

It was already light that May morning when Soli and Dolores made their way to the castle grounds. Soli's first day working there consisted of obeying her mother's orders. *Take this there! Bring that here!* Dolores was in her glory.

After a week they fell into a more amicable rhythm. Soli worked on chores in one area of the grounds, and her mother in another. They worked according to explicit instructions the *señor* left Dolores, preparing gardens and clearing walkways. She even gave orders to the workmen restoring the castle.

Soon, even Dolores had to admit that there were things Soli didn't do all that badly.

"Don Ramón is a very practical man," Dolores explained to Soli one day as they weeded. "He told me 'No silly flowers. Only vegetables.'" Soli could hear the admiration in her mother's voice.

"Where is he now?" she asked.

"In Madrid. On business. He is a busy man. Doesn't have time to waste in this silly village."

"Then why is he spending all this money on fixing an old castle?" Soli found it romantic, but she knew that was not a sentiment Dolores would share.

Her mother paused and Soli sensed her thoughts in conflict. Then Dolores bent over again. "Get back to work."

The *señor* finally arrived in June. Dolores was particularly tense that day. Soli decided to stay out of her way.

Her mother was inside the groundskeeper's cottage cooking and cleaning in preparation for Don Ramón's stay, and the workmen were busy replacing stones in the inner courtyard. Soli wandered off to work behind the south wall, where some ugly weeds grew between the cracks of the stones. The wall overlooked a peaceful tree-lined slope and stream. The tower on her left was partly crumbled, while the one on the right was still quite intact. She remembered coming here with her cousins, play-acting the story of the bad man. Fernan would be the ogre, chasing the screaming girls around.

Soli moved her basket to the right as she spied another clump of stubborn greenery, then straightened to stretch her back and wipe sweat off her forehead. From the corner of her eye, she saw a man watching her from the tower window. Embarrassed, she gathered the basket and scurried to the front of the castle where the cottage and vegetable patch were. She had hardly reached the low stone wall when she heard her mother say, "Where have you been? Dawdling somewhere? Do I have to tell you what to do every minute of the day?"

Soli saw the man from the tower, tall and tanned, stride through the castle gate. "Dolores, don't you ever get tired of the sound of your own voice?"

Dolores whirled.

"Well, I ... it's just that she ..." Her eyes bounced from her daughter to the man.

To Soli's relief, he said no more. She didn't look up, but she sensed him giving her the once-over, then walk away. Soli put the basket down, physically preparing herself for her mother's verbal abuse, but none came.

"You were pulling weeds," Dolores said, her voice thick. "That's good." Then she e walked away. Soli was suddenly overwhelmed with pity for her.

———

Don Ramón came and went, but when he arrived, he spent most of his time was spent in the cottage. Parts of the castle would remain in ruins as it was too costly to restore them, but enough was being repaired to give a good idea of its former glory. One of many built during the wars between the Moors and the Christians, it was compact and consisted of four round towers and four joining walls, creating a courtyard in the middle. No one knew what Don Ramón planned to do with the place. Sell it? Rent it out for weddings, films, concerts? Convert it into a museum? He had already amassed quite a collection of medieval objects, including tools and instruments for farming, cooking, even war.

One day, when her mother was busy and the *señor* was nowhere in sight, Soli went exploring. She started in the main hall, which she remembered as being full of rubble. Now it was full of light and furnished with a few dark, rustic chairs around a table, and metal objects hanging on the walls.

She tried the door that led to the south tower. It wasn't locked and, recently oiled, it swung open easily. She looked up, expecting to see the crumbling steps she used to scramble up, but saw new, wooden ones instead. She climbed them gingerly. As she reached the top, the new wooden floor gleamed under light filtering in through the window.

As her eyes adjusted, she perceived Don Ramón in the shadows. She started for the stairs.

"Don't go," he said softly, holding out his hand. "I don't mind. Please come." She turned and stepped forward. "Look," he said, taking her lightly by the shoulders and directing her toward the window.

She could see the slope of trees and the silvery thread of stream below. In the distance beyond meadows, stood the remains of an old stone building. "Here," he said. "Use these." He handed her a pair of binoculars. She took them and leaned into the window. He was standing behind her, his hands on the walls on either side of her, encircling her. She inhaled his scent of leather mixed with tobacco.

"That's an old monastery. The lord of this castle built it hundreds of years ago to thank God for helping him win back the land across the river. In those days, on the Feast of the Assumption, they would carry the statue of the Virgin to the monastery. In the evening they would return, dark monks riding white horses, singing Gregorian chants, and carrying colourful lanterns. They would float the Virgin across the river, her crown and robes glistening in the moonlight."

She stood, petrified.

"Do you like the view?"

She nodded.

"Come." He stepped back, gently pulling her by the shoulders, and took the binoculars from her. He steered her shoulders to face the walls. "Do you know what those instruments are for?"

Hooks and bars, ropes and whips. Rings, clasps, screws, knobs, pulleys. It was a strange assortment.

"Yes," she lied, not wanting to sound ignorant. She felt faint. She looked at his face in the shadows for the first time. He was staring icily at the wall. She had the impression that he seemed to be engaged in an inner struggle. He suddenly reeled backward. "You had better go."

She ran and didn't stop until she was out of the castle grounds. She sat against the trunk of a tree to catch her breath, hugging her knees tightly.

Soli and her mother had been white-washing walls in the castle for weeks, and Don Ramon was pushing them to get the job done Meanwhile, crates and boxes kept arriving from Madrid and Barcelona, even some from Paris.

"I asked him what the big rush was for," Dolores said, "and he told me 'For the Feast of the Virgin, of course', and burst out laughing. Who can understand these men."

Dolores shook her head and smiled. In the past few weeks, her mood could almost be called cheerful. She had been arranging her hair, and Soli had even heard her humming.

Every August 15th, the towns celebrated the Feast of the

Assumption of the Virgin Mary. A grand procession from the church was led by the float with a statue of the Virgin dressed in the opulent blue and white robe and crown. After the procession and Mass, fireworks, eating, drinking, singing and dancing was held at the fairgrounds and continued well into the wee hours. The festivities continued for days as young people visited friends and cousins in different towns.

The year of 1976 marked the first time since the civil war that the festivities would be held without a dictatorship. As the *fiestas* drew nearer, the town bustled with families coming back to the village from Madrid and other big cities. Young people like Fernan and Pati were ecstatic to see the young *madrileños* but tried hard not to act like country bumpkins around them. Pati found a new romantic interest from Madrid. "I'll get to see him a lot in the fall when Fernan goes to university," she confided to Soli one evening as they were washing dishes at Espe's house. "I have the perfect boyfriend for you. He's a friend of Paco's."

Soli let her cousin prattle on. She still could not forget that strange afternoon with Don Ramón in the tower, the way he had touched her, firmly but also like a caress, his voice soft yet commanding. He had seemed attracted to her yet pushed her away. She was both eager and afraid to see him again.

On the Monday before the *fiesta*, Dolores and Soli arrived at the castle. They were amazed at the transformation. The courtyard was spectacular with colourful lanterns hanging along the walls, large clay pots filled with red and white flowers every few meters. Flags and decorations adorned the place. When they entered one of the bright rooms they had white-washed, they found a large, canopied bed covered with a dazzling red embroidered bedspread. The curtains matched the spread and shimmered in the morning light.

"Is he planning to move in here after all the work we did getting the cottage in order? He never mentioned a thing to me." Dolores sounded hurt.

"Maybe he's expecting guests," Soli offered.

Dolores was no longer wearing the happy expression of these past few weeks. Soli wondered in panic what she had done wrong this time.

Her mother gave her a sharp look. "Do you remember that story about the bad man *Abuela* and I used to tell you?"

Soli bowed her head, "Yes," she whispered.

"What do you remember about that story?" Her mother crossed her arms.

"The bad man kidnapped bad girls to ... to punish them."

"There is another thing *Abuela* never wanted you to know." Dolores's voice turned to ice. "The other version of the story is that those girls were not kidnapped."

Soli was puzzled.

"How do you think they got here?" Dolores said.

"I ... I don't know."

"They came by choice. Of their own accord. That's the kind of girls they were."

Dolores marched out, leaving Soli shaken and not really knowing why.

When Soli was six, she and her mother went to visit her father and Uncle Pablo in Frankfurt. They were both working in construction and bartending on weekends, like many Spaniards did in the sixties to earn money. They lived in an apartment with several other men. Since her father shared his room with his brother, Pablo went to stay with his girlfriend, Ursula, who Dolores referred to as *la guarra alemana* (the German slut), so his brother and wife could have some privacy.

One of the flatmates, whom Soli was instructed to call Onkel Volker, spent his evenings in the darkened living room listening to the radio and drinking beer, while the others went out. Volker was nice to Soli, giving her chewing gum, or presents like a little plastic doll, and playing games.

One evening, Dolores shooed her daughter out of the bedroom, saying "Sit with your Onkel Volker. He likes little girls." A challenge rang in her voice, which both frightened and intrigued Soli.

When Dolores later came into the living room and saw what Onkel Volker was doing to Soli, she grabbed her daughter's arm and slapped her. *Guarra,* she called her. She said nothing to the man. Soli's father stood in the doorway, confused. Dolores screamed at him. "You prefer to live with perverts than with your own family!" She yanked Soli's arm. "We're getting out of here."

Soli's father bought their tickets for an overnight train home. They had to wait a long time in the draughty station. He tried awkwardly to make conversation with his wife while Soli pretended to sleep on a bench. Dolores's attitude had softened slightly. As she tucked a coat around the little girl, Soli heard her mother whisper *"Pobrecita,"* but Soli knew she had done something terribly wrong and that was why they were leaving. That was the last time Soli saw her father.

———

The 15th finally arrived. The statue of the Virgin looked glorious in her magnificent robes high up on her float. The procession was said to be grander than any other in living memory. Even Pati could find nothing cynical to say.

When the day cooled off, a band set up and everyone headed to the fairgrounds located at the foot of the hill just below the castle road. Soli, with Abuela, Esperanza and her little cousins, met an irate group of ladies, accompanied by the parish priest, hurrying from the direction of the church. Someone had stolen the Virgin's crown and robes!

"That's what happens with so much liberty!" shouted one of the women.

"Yes!" another added. *"¡Una cosa es la democracia, y otra la desvergüenza!"* One thing is democracy, and another is shamelessness!

"Probably some of those young *sinvergüenzas* from Madrid," the priest said.

They continued their search for the Virgin's clothes, while Soli's group approached the fairgrounds. Pati had lent Soli a blue and white flowered summer dress, and Espe had helped do her hair and even made up her eyes. *"Preciosa,"* her aunt said with pride. "You never know who you might meet today."

Euphoria reigned. The young people had heard about the Virgin's stolen clothes, and they had already made up a song about it. Everyone was laughing, shouting, and crashing drunkenly into one another, singing *"¿Quién ha robado la ropa de la Virgen? ¡La pobre se ha quedado en pelotas y le da mucha vergüenza!"* Who stole the Virgin's clothes? She's naked and embarrassed.

Soli had never felt so pretty. Everyone was smiling at her. Shortly before midnight Pati and her new friends decided to go swimming in a nearby lake. Skinny dipping, Pati said, like they do in other countries. Soli was flattered to be included.

As the group danced, shrieked, and laughed to the parking lot, Soli looked at the castle road. She was surprised to see Don Ramón there watching her. Instinctively, she knew he was waiting for her. Soli let go of Pati's hand and drifted towards him.

He turned.

She followed.

"Where are you going, Soli?" Pati called.

But Soli, focused on the man ahead of her, didn't hear. As they entered the castle gate, the fireworks started in the fairgrounds. Ramón stopped and picked something up. "Put this on."

It was the Virgin's magnificent cloak. Soli put it on, as she had months before. He adjusted it around her shoulders and placed the crown on her head.

"Now is the time. Walk, with pride, my virgin queen," he said in a commanding voice. They crossed the courtyard aglow with lanterns to the south tower.

When they got to the top of the tower stairs, he guided her to the window, gently removed the cloak, unzipped her dress, and asked in a hoarse whisper, "Have you been bad?"

Soli bowed her head and with a great sense of relief, admitted, "Yes."

"I will cleanse you," he said and lifted her right arm to a rope on the wall and looped it around her wrist. "Then, you will sin with me."

"Yes," she said, as he tugged the knot tight.

"But never worry," he whispered in her left ear, as he took the other wrist. "I will always be here to cleanse you."

"Yes." She imagined the ecstatic merry-go-round of sin and penance.

"Again and again and again."

With the first bite of the whip, she saw the monks chanting as they rode their white horses toward her.

GAZPACHO

Anita Haas

Image by Тикунова from pixabay.com.

INGREDIENTS:

2 pounds of ripe, peeled tomatoes
1 peeled cucumber,
1 chopped green onion
1 green pepper
2 chopped garlic cloves
3 ½ oz stale, white bread, with crusts removed, soaked briefly in water then compressed with a paper towel to remove excess.
2/3 cup extra virgin olive oil
¼ cup red wine vinegar
Salt, pepper, cumin (to taste)

DIRECTIONS:

Purée all ingredients. Chill and serve either in bowls or glasses.

We Were Neighbors

Shai Afsai

Jewish Culture Festival — Poland

When I heard about Jewish culture festivals in Poland that were not only organized but also attended by many non-Jews, I was intrigued. Before the decimation of World War II, Poland had the largest Jewish population in Europe. Those Jews who survived the Holocaust and remained in Poland suffered persecution under the subsequent anti-semitic communist government, reducing their numbers even further. Now Poles were celebrating Jewish history? A friend of mine living part-time in Kraków told me I had to see this for myself.

In 2019, I traveled from my home in Rhode Island, United States, to Kraków, where Jews made up almost a quarter of the city's residents prior to World War II. I was headed to the 29th Jewish Culture Festival: ten days of concerts, film screenings, walking tours, photo exhibits, literary programs, Torah classes, panel discussions, lectures, and culinary workshops attended by thousands of people from Poland and abroad.

Many Jewish structures still stand in Kazimierz — the area of Kraków that Polish King Casimir the Great invited Jews to settle in during the 14th century — but after two successive totalitarian regimes, they are now largely empty of Jewish occupants. In the 1930s, there were about 3 million Jews in Poland, about 10 percent of the population. By the end of World War II, in the space of less than six years, 90 percent of them had died at the hands of the Nazis and their accomplices. Today, Poland's core Jewish community numbers just 4,500 individuals, according to the Institute for Jewish Policy Research.

The Jewish Culture Festival's founders and organizers, and most of its attendees, are non-Jewish Poles. An American Jew who hears about a Jewish culture festival in Poland founded, organized, and mostly attended by non-Jews might think negatively of it as cultural appropriation or some sort of whitewashing of history. But the more people I met in Kraków and the more I saw of Kazimierz, the more I wanted to understand why so many non-Jews in Poland were constructively invested in learning about, experiencing, and promoting Jewish culture.

"It is very difficult to answer, 'Why are you doing this?' It is like answering, 'Why do you breathe and live?' I am a man who is aware he was born in the largest Jewish cemetery in the world, but also that six years of Shoah [the Holocaust] cannot eclipse a thousand years," Janusz Makuch, the festival's non-Jewish founder and director, told me. We were chatting in Cheder, a Middle Eastern-themed café situated in one of Kazimierz's former Jewish houses of study and prayer.

"When I started putting together a Jewish festival at age twenty-eight, it was the only one in Poland. Now there are over forty Jewish culture festivals. I felt the obligation to plant the seed. It came from a deep responsibility to memory, but also from deep fascination with and love of Jewish culture," Makuch said. "When I started to plant the seed, I noticed that many [Polish] people — especially, but not only, young people — long to learn, each for their own reasons, about Jewish culture, which is also a part of their culture. Come on! We were living a thousand years with Jewish people on the same soil as neighbors!"

Kazimierz is a mix of old structures and modern ones, of cobblestone streets and pavement. On Friday evening and Saturday morning, I walked to Sabbath services at the Isaac Synagogue (Synagoga Izaaka), which was built in the 17th century and is one of the seven remaining synagogue buildings in Kazimierz. It was full of worshippers, many of whom were visitors from Israel, and the services were joyous and lively.

Yet as my eyes wandered around the large sanctuary, my mind wandered to the many Jews who had prayed here over the centuries, and I felt moments of tremendous sadness. Most of the people who prayed here in 1939, when the Nazis invaded, perished in the Holocaust. Were it not for the Israeli visitors there that Sabbath, the building would have been mostly empty.

The first festival event I attended at Kraków's Galicia Jewish Museum (Żydowskie Muzeum Galicja) was a guided tour through Chuck Fishman's photography exhibit "Regeneration: Jewish Life in Poland," which focused on the mid-1970s to the present. The tour was led by museum educator Anna Wencel. Afterward, I met her in the museum's courtyard, and she told me about her interest in Jews from a young age and about her work at the museum since 2008.

"I come from a small town near Oświęcim (Auschwitz). I grew up in the same house my family lived in for four generations. I knew Jews had shops and lived in areas of the town. Before the [Second World] War, 500 people, one-fourth of the town, were Jewish. When I was eight — it was in 1989 — by chance I went into a local Jewish cemetery with a friend. We saw tombstones, but we could not read the inscriptions. One tombstone had a crown and we thought maybe it was the grave of a king or queen. It seemed like something from a fairy tale," Wencel recounted. "I told my grandmother what we found, and she explained to me that it was a Jewish cemetery. My grandmother was born in 1923. She refused to tell me anything about the war, but she talked a lot about the interwar period [between World Wars I and II], as if everything was better before the war. It was too traumatic for her."

Wencel's fascination with Jewish culture and history eventually led her to enroll in the Jewish Studies department at Kraków's Jagiellonian University.

"When I came to Kraków, I went to Kazimierz from time to time, and on my way home I often went by tramway, passing Ghetto Heroes Square. I saw tangible places, materials, and objects of the Jewish past in Kraków and in other places. I learned there was a department of Jewish Studies at Jagiellonian University and applied," she said.

"I studied Jewish women writing poetry in Yiddish during the interwar years. It was a lot of translation. I did five years of Jewish

Studies in the history department. When I was at university, there was a project to translate inscriptions from Jewish tombstones. I went back to that cemetery in my hometown and found the grave with the crown, now being able to read the epitaphs in Hebrew. I learned that the man buried there is Moshe Huppert and the crown is a *keter shem tov,* the crown of a good reputation."

Being a non-Jewish guide at a Jewish museum has its tensions, Wencel told me.

"There are people for whom their job is their passion. I am in that group. I do not believe in dividing things into 'This is *my* story; this is *their* story.' At the end of the day, we are all human. At the museum, I often get asked if I am Jewish by Jewish people, implying that it is not my story to tell. And some Christians ask the same thing with suspicion, implying a non-Jewish person cannot have actual knowledge in this field — 'How can you know this?' Sometimes it gets a little bit antisemitic with non-Jewish visitors, implying that they want to listen to 'a real Jew,' someone representing this 'exotic' culture," Wencel said.

The next event I attended at the museum was a talk by Paul Schneller, a Swiss veterinarian specializing in exotic animals who is also a professional photographer. In "About Polish Jews: See You Next Year in Kraków," Schneller discussed his family's taboo surrounding his Jewish great-grandfather, Saul Chaim Grunfest, who was a communist, a friend of Lenin, and the first Jewish Social Democratic Party member in Switzerland. Neither Grunfest's communism nor his Jewishness were spoken of in Schneller's home, though it was clear from his name that he was a Jew.

Schneller, cheerful, bespectacled, and with a mop of wavy hair, met me for a drink the next day at a restaurant in Kazimierz.

"I am very attached to Kraków and Poland, but Kraków is not representative of Poland," he said. "It is an unusual place. When you first come to Kraków, you just see the tourism here, but there is something more and deeper here about Jewish life. The tourism itself is superficial, but it allows for a conversation to take place, like we are having now."

Schneller continued more somberly. "There are more non-Jews active here in Jewish life than Jews. The Jewish Culture Festival is run by non-Jews. The director of the Galicia Jewish Museum is not Jewish.

This Jewish life here would not exist without the non-Jewish people. When I ask Polish people about this activity, they say, 'I feel a gap. I feel there is something missing. We have to fill this gap.' Jewish absence in Poland has been described as a phantom limb. My interpretation is that with their interest in Jews, Polish people are involved in healing. It is a possible therapy — probably not conscious, but subconscious — to deal with a phantom pain, the trauma of the Nazis. They miss the Jews. They had a thousand-year history living alongside the Jews, and in six years the Nazis wiped it out."

Another event I attended at the Galicia Jewish Museum was a presentation and panel discussion about the pictures and figurines of the "Lucky Jew" that are sold throughout Poland. There are quite a few artistic variations on the theme, but one common portrait depicts a bearded man dressed in pre-World War II Eastern European Jewish garb counting gold coins. Another shows a bearded Jew with a quill pen recording numbers in a ledger. Such items are thought to bring good luck, especially with finances, and are hung in homes and shops across the country. If this were done in the United States, the trend would be rightly seen as expressing anti-Jewish prejudice. In Poland, it is more complicated.

When the event ended, I turned to the woman seated next to me and asked for her thoughts. The woman, Margaret Krawecka, a Polish-born artist and architectural and interior design consultant who lives in Canada, proposed that we go to the museum's café to talk, and this ended up being among the most emotional conversations I had in Kraków.

"Polish people have intergenerational trauma from witnessing the abuse and destruction of their friends and neighbors," Krawecka said. "Non-Jews are trying to come to terms with the fact that about one-fifth of the population was wiped out. Some Polish people helped Jews at risk to their lives, some collaborated [with the Nazis], but most just watched, paralyzed by the fear and terror spread by the Nazi occupiers. There is a feeling of helplessness and maybe also a confused sense of guilt. This country is still very deeply affected by the trauma of World War II. Even me. I was born in 1978, many years after the war, and still the weight is heavy. It is the memory."

Polish people cope with the trauma and memory, which remain connected to Jews, in various ways, she noted.

"Some Polish people seem like they are not ready to move on. Of course, they have to. You can never forget what happened, but you also have to move forward, without forgetting," Krawecka said. "A lot of people have an existential void, a sense of nostalgia, a missing of another time and place. In some strange way, perhaps these figurines of Jews, these lucky charms, are an attempt to bring back the past. There are so many complexities, so many layers. It is almost like the word *Jew* has become a symbol."

I found myself repeatedly returning to the Galicia Jewish Museum throughout my visit. Days at the festival, which was held in late-June, were sun-drenched and humid, and after seeing me numerous times, the museum's director, Jakub Nowakowski, joked that I must like its air conditioning. Now forty, Nowakowski, an energetic man who sported a stylish and long dark beard that would make Theodor Herzl, the iconic founder of political Zionism, proud, has been heading the Galicia Jewish Museum since 2010. We finally found time for an extended conversation in the museum one evening, and I asked him for his perspective on non-Jewish efforts to learn about contemporary Jewish culture and preserve the memory of Jews in Poland.

"If you go to the small towns, which you don't see in the media often, you also see that many of them are interested in Jewish culture and history and organize Jewish festivals as well. If you go to the small villages that have these festivals, [you see] there is no money made there. It *costs* them money," Nowakowski said. "Why are people in these remote areas spending money to renovate synagogues and have Jewish festivals? Why do teachers come here? Why do they come to spend their vacations studying in Kraków? They are not doing it for money."

Nowakowski felt there were several reasons.

"Is it because we feel guilty? Of course some Poles feel guilty for what was done to the Jews. Others just miss the Jews, who are still alive in the memories of their parents and grandparents. But there is also the pride of coming from the multicultural world that existed here. People look around, see homogeneity, and look for something different. It is about memory. It is about finding peace and moving forward. We live in the post-Holocaust space in a way no other country does. Traces of Jewish life and death exist so close to each other," he said.

During my stay in Kraków, I got to know some of the festival volunteers, called *machers,* including best friends Joanna Chojnacka and Dominika Kołodziej. The two women, in their twenties, met me for lunch one day at Hevre, a former *beth midrash* (Jewish house of study and prayer) that is owned by the Gmina Żydowska, Kraków's official religious Jewish community, which leases it out as a trendy restaurant and bar. Exposed pre-Holocaust Hebrew calligraphy and paintings of holy sites in the land of Israel still adorn its walls. I was troubled that this was the fate of a once-sacred location, and that more was not being done to safeguard its religious history. But with so few Jews left in Kraków, and with other Jewish structures requiring preservation and restoration, it may make sense for the Gmina Żydowska to use this one as a source of revenue.

Kołodziej was completing a master's degree in Jewish Studies at Jagiellonian University.

"I always had an interest in Jewish history, but more of the interwar period, because I felt it was not studied much," she said. "I was especially interested in the music and the movies of the interwar period, many of which were made by Jews, especially in Warsaw. I always liked hearing songs in Yiddish. Warsaw has a specific dialect, and most of it is from before the war. Many of the words are in Yiddish."

She described the recent revitalization of Jewish life in Kraków.

"It has become more and more normal to see Jewish people here. There is curiosity, maybe from tourists, but in Kraków, people know there are Jewish people here, and they fit in the area and no one is surprised anymore. I feel it is very specific to Kraków," Kołodziej said. "We are used to seeing Orthodox people rushing to synagogue for Friday night. It is natural for us now."

Chojnacka, who also majored in Jewish Studies, had written a novel titled *Szpagat* (an insult in the Varsavian dialect for a well-educated person) about a Jewish tailor who returns to Warsaw after the war and finds the Jewish quarter gone.

"I had this idea four years ago," she explained. "One of the reasons I chose Jewish Studies was to learn about Jewish life and to learn some

Yiddish. I wanted my writing to be as authentic as possible. It is impossible, but I said, 'I will try.' At the time I did not tell my professors why I wanted Jewish Studies, because it is quite unusual that you write about something that does not belong to you. I cannot consider myself Jewish, and I am writing from the perspective of the main character, who is a Jew. I was worried people would say, 'It is not your thing. You should not write it.' But then I started saying to myself, 'Then who will write it?' I wanted to tell the story of the Jewish people of my city, who are also my people."

In answer to the question of why so many Poles are interested in Jewish culture, Chojnacka took a moment to reflect. "I think Polish people still miss Jewish culture. We were neighbors. We were very close. More and more we miss it. People want to feel it, but it is very hard to feel it authentically. We are still searching for the way to show it," she said. "In Kraków, we still have the buildings and the synagogues, so it is easier. There is a Jewish quarter. I feel the Jewish Culture Festival is doing this very well. It is a very good way to show people Jewish culture, modern Jewish culture and with a focus on Israel. We are searching for something Jewish in Poland, and this is the way to learn something authentic."

As I experienced it, Kraków's Jewish Culture Festival, with its many and varied offerings, does indeed authentically, and sincerely and respectfully, present contemporary Jewish culture, while also grappling with the history of Jews in Poland and current Jewish-related issues in the country. Alongside festival offerings in Polish or in English, there were many speakers, authors, cantors, singers, musicians, artists, and religious figures who were Israeli and spoke or performed in Hebrew. This was intentional.

"Most importantly, I know that Israel is the center of Jewish life," Makuch, the Jewish Culture Festival's founder and director, told me. "It is a festival dedicated to contemporary Jewish culture and life, which is centered in Israel. Israel is also a center of *my* life. Being Jewish, *you* are connected to Israel. Israel is *my* country and chosen land too. Jerusalem is *my* city. One year ago, I was awarded the title of Yakir Yisrael [Friend of Israel] and was hosted by [Israeli] President Rivlin. I am a non-Jewish director of a Jewish festival. I am a Polish Zionist."

HONEY CAKE
Shai Afsai

This recipe for honey cake from Poland is by Polish novelist Joanna Chojnacka, who put her own twist on one found in *The Light Jewish Cookbook: Recipes from Around the World for Weight Loss and Health*, by Sylvie Jouffa and Annick Champetier de Ribes.

INGREDIENTS:

1/4 cup granulated sugar
2 tsp vanilla extract or vanilla sugar
1 2/3 cup white flour
2 tsp baking powder
1 tbsp canola oil
1/3 cup honey
2 egg whites
Pinch of salt
Pinch of cinnamon or cardamom
½ cup strong coffee
2 tbsp ground almonds
Almond flakes

DIRECTIONS:

1. Add honey to the hot coffee and stir until smooth.
2. Add the flour, oil, ground almonds, cinnamon and/or cardamom, sugar, vanilla and baking powder to the mixture.
3. In a separate bowl, whisk the egg whites with a pinch of salt to a stiff froth, then gently stir the mixture into the batter.
4. Pour batter into a square cake tin (I used a 26 x15 cm/10.2 x 6 inches). Sprinkle the top with flaked almonds.
5. Bake for 35 minutes at 170 degrees C/345 F.
6. Sprinkle the finished cake with icing (confectioner's) sugar if desired.

THE HOLIDAY COMMITTEE

WILLIAM JOHN ROSTRON

Kingdom of Matilda

MEETING 1

"Do you know what happened on October 10, 1582?" the Minister of Antiquities, Alexander Crowden, asked.

"I'm guessing some obscure leader's birth or perhaps a great victory in battle? Besides, I don't care. That gibberish is your bailiwick," the Minister of Finance, Francis Wallingford, grumbled. "You know the accumulation of useless information is the reason for your hiring. No, excuse me, for you being appointed to your illustrious and useless position."

"How about a little respect? I don't blame you for your uselessness, Mr. Minister of Finance. We live in a country where the king makes all the decisions about everything."

"But I advise him about how to make those decisions correctly."

"Big whoop. The two of you make a mistake, and he'll take another billion out of his back pocket to cover your screw-up."

"So says the Minister of Antiquities for a country that is only eleven months old. Hell, I have toothpaste older than this country."

"Excuse me, but I was hired for my knowledge of *other* countries' histories. I know that I could relate the entire history of *our* country on a postage stamp, but that's not why I am here."

"Let's see you do it."

"Do what?"

"I made a little handout to summarize our history for those who might not remember. Please read it."

"If I must. However, we do need to get to our task."

"*Our* history is a starting point for what we need to do today."

"Hand me that paper, and let's see what you have."

The Minister of Finance started reading.

In 2019, Joseph James Simpson won the largest lottery in United States history—over $1 billion. He then went to a casino in Macau because none in America would cover a bet of $1 billion on Stony Brook University to win the NCAA championship during March Madness. Of course, rumors were that he somehow used his money to rig the result. However, they were never proven.

Crowden turned to the recording secretary, Elizabeth Parker-Smythe. "Betty, cross out that last sentence. It was pure speculation, correct?"

"I know who signs my paycheck."

"Continue."

So Simpson, er...excuse me, King Joseph, buys Little Ragged Island, the smallest island in the Bahamas, for $11 million, but only on the condition that he would be allowed to declare it a sovereign nation—the Kingdom of Matilda, so named for his mother.

COVID-19 hit in 2020, and this little island had more than enough people who wanted to emigrate there. So, King Joseph created the most modern location on the planet—moving sidewalks, a monorail, a hurricane-proof domed stadium for all sports, luxury apartments, and more.

"The people worked hard to make this country what it is, and now they need a break," said the Minister of Finance Wallingford. It was not actually his name, but King Joseph had renamed his closest aides with names that sounded like they were members of the House of Lords.

"And that's why we are here," Crowden said.

"The two of us are to decide on nine national holidays for the Kingdom of Matilda. I will provide worldwide political and cultural context. By the way, Francis, may I call you Frank?"

"If I must have this abomination of a name, I prefer Wally. How about you?"

"You can call me Al, and please don't start singing."

"I don't get it."

"You know, the Paul Simon song, 'You Can Call Me Al'?"

"I have no idea what you are talking about. Old songs and old things mean nothing. Money is all that matters, um, Al?"

"Our work is cut out for us because holidays are about recognizing the past greatness of a person or an event."

"That's your expertise. But where do we start?"

"With a calendar."

"We have calendars all over the place. "

"We are charged with starting something totally new so we could use the Chinese, Muslim, or Jewish calendar."

"Why on earth would we do that? Why not just use the Western calendar?"

"Which one? The Julian would be interesting, quite groundbreaking in its use of solar calculating but with the corrections of the Gregorian changes."

"Al, do you realize that you are rambling nonsense? Could you please explain?"

"Julius Caesar created the first modern solar calendar. It was extremely accurate for 45 B.C. That was before politics got involved. Legend has it that Julius took a day from February and added it to—can you guess?"

"No."

"July, the month named after him."

"That's wrong in so many ways."

"It gets worse. When Caesar's adopted son became emperor, he was not to be outdone by dear old adopted dad. So, he took another day from February, added it to the eighth month, and then renamed it after himself, Augustus Caesar."

"So that's why February is so short on days."

"Yes and no. No January and February existed in the original calendar before Julius Caesar created his version. There were only ten months, and the year began in March. Therefore, February was the last month added. It got no respect."

"But when they made January 1 the first day of the year, everything worked out, right?"

"Not really. September, October, November, and December actually mean the seventh, eighth, ninth, and tenth months in Latin. It was never changed even when they became the ninth, tenth, eleventh, and twelfth months."

"This is getting entirely too complicated. Our job is to come up with holidays. Just finish the story."

"The story does end with a holiday decision."

"Huh?"

"Most of Western civilization accepted the calendar for over 1,500 years. However, many still celebrate the new year in March. Eventually, many New Year's celebrations took place the last week of March, making April the first full month of the year. This made no sense since January had been the first month of the year for all that time."

"What did they do?"

"Remember my first question to you today: what happened on October 10, 1564? The Church, the only power in Europe, realized that not only was New Year's Day screwed up, but a slight error made by Julius Caesar was now multiplied by 1,500 years, and months were now happening in different seasons. To the Church, this was important because this meant that all their holidays, especially Easter, were thrown off. So, they fixed it by fiddling around with leap years and made it work. That's the calendar we have today."

"Then everything was perfect?"

"Well, no. They needed help to make up for mistakes of 1,500 years, which brings us to October 10, 1582. The Church decreed that October

5 through 14 in 1582 would not occur. People went to bed on Thursday, October 4, and woke up on Friday, October 15."

"And I thought daylight saving was confusing."

"The second part is more to the point. New Year's was officially changed to January 1. However, many did not get the memo. After celebrating through the end of March, they were ready for the new year on April 1. What do you think people were called when they ran around the streets celebrating?"

"April Fools!"

"You got it."

MEETING 2

"Wally, our last meeting was fun, but we must make progress. All we agreed on was following the United States calendar and not having April Fools as a holiday. So that's why I've brought my nephew, Jeremy. He's going to give us a fresh set of eyes."

"Why?"

"So, we settle on the national holidays before we celebrate our centennial!"

"Alright, let's start with the Washington and Lincoln birthdays," Al said.

"Who are they?" Jeremy asked.

"Really?" Al said.

"Education is not what it used to be," Wally said with a snicker.

"Washington was our first president, and Lincoln was president during the Civil War," Al said.

"He was not the first president of Matilda. In fact, we never had a president, or for that matter, a civil war," Jeremy said. "We are not America. Therefore, we do not have to recreate the American holidays."

"But 95 percent of our population were American residents two years ago," Al said.

"From where in the United States?"

"What do you mean?"

"If they came from the Northeast, they would expect to have Presidents' Week off. If they were from the Midwest, they might expect either Washington's or Lincoln's only. If they were from the Deep South, they celebrated Robert E. Lee's birthday on January 19, almost until the end of the 20th century," Jeremy said.

"I give up. No presidents. In fact, we can do away with Fourth of July, Flag Day, Veterans Day, and Memorial Day," Wally said. As director of finance, he was looking to cut the days people were paid for not working.

"That's not a good idea," Jeremy said.

Al agreed, though he was surprised that the twenty-something favored these four holidays. "Veterans Day started as the celebration of the end of World War I on the eleventh hour of the eleventh day of the eleventh month in 1918. It then became a celebration of all veterans of the armed forces."

"Then what is Memorial Day?" Jeremy said.

"Memorial Day is for veterans who died while defending their country. Big difference," Al answered.

"But we have no veterans. We don't even have an army," Wally said.

"Maybe we don't have armed forces in Matilda, but we do have veterans. They may have served elsewhere, but we should honor them. We may need them if we ever fight an aggressive neighbor."

Jeremy had a solution. "How about one holiday—Veterans Memorial Day, and we can eliminate all the rest."

Al and Wally nodded.

"Do you know who pays your salary?" Wally asked with a smile.

"I'm not getting any salary," Jeremy said.

"If you ever want to get a good job in this country, you better remember who decides what happens here," Wally said.

Jeremy's face lit up with a new thought. "See how you like these ideas. Instead of July 4, let's celebrate 'Founding Day' when King Joseph bought the island from the Bahamas and created this new country."

"Great idea," Al exclaimed.

"Instead of Presidents' Day, we celebrate King Joseph's Birthday on March 1, his birthday."

"I gotta say, nephew, you have a knack for kissing up to the boss. Wait, Betty, please change that last statement to 'You understand the needs of the country to honor his majesty.' Delete the first part of my statement, the 'kissing up' part."

"Flag Day could be honoring our flag."

"Jeremy, now you have jumped the shark. Our flag is a picture of King Joseph on a blue background. That is too much."

"Did you really say that, Uncle Wally?"

"Betty, strike that last statement and replace it with, 'Matilda Flag Day sounds like a great idea. Let's see if we have room for it in our calendar when we are done."

"Now we must consider Martin Luther King Day, Juneteenth, and Columbus Day, or is it now Indigenous People's Day? Al, what do you think?"

"This won't be easy. Those days were controversial when they were first suggested."

"But we're not in America. Isn't that what you always say to me, Uncle Wally?"

"Al, help us out here."

"It's nearly my nap time. Let's pick this up tomorrow."

MEETING 3

"We have a guest," Al announced.

"This is my girlfriend, Lucy. I thought she could help with our discussions," Jeremy indicated the young woman beside him.

"We discussed political holidays at our last meeting, Lucy, so I've prepared a fact sheet for your perusal."

"For our what?"

"Peruse...for you to look at. Is that simple enough, Jeremy? Education really has dropped off," Al said with a groan.

"We're getting off track early," Wally said. "What about Columbus?"

"In a sense, he is our real founder. His first known landing was in the Bahamas. Perhaps, even on this very island. Wouldn't that be special?" Al said.

Wally agreed. "It's a story that connects our history to the history of the world. What could be better?"

"Columbus also led ultimately biological globalization."

"Biological what?" Jeremy asked.

"It means plants and animals were transferred to places they had never been. For example, the Europeans brought horses, pigs, cattle, goats, and sheep to the Americas," Al said.

"And rats," Lucy spoke for the first time.

"They stowed away on the ships, but that's to be expected," Al said.

"Is it?" Lucy said, smirking. "We didn't have rats, and now we do. That's okay by you, Mr. Historian?"

"A small price to pay for all those other animals," Al snapped.

"Who decided that it was a small price? Columbus or the Taino, who were here first?

Al didn't answer.

"Didn't the Europeans also bring wheat, rye, and barley?" Wally chimed in.

"We gave you back potatoes, sweet potatoes, tomatoes, peanuts, pumpkins, squashes, pineapples, and chili peppers. However, my favorite on the list is tobacco, so all you colonizers could get cancer."

"Am I detecting a bit of animosity from you, Lucy?" Wally remarked.

"How observant of you, Wally," Al said. "Lucy, Jeremy obviously brought you here for a reason. So, let's hear it."

"My real name isn't Lucy. Like all you pompous asses, I took a new name when King Joseph took our island."

"Excuse me, he bought it fair and square from the Bahamian government," Wally snapped.

"What right did they have to sell it to him?" Lucy's voice rose in a challenge.

"Wally, calm down. Let's hear what she has to say." Al nodded at Lucy. "Proceed."

"I took the name *Lukku-Cairi,* which is our name for our people, the original people that Columbus came upon. You two bigshots left out the most important gifts brought to us: disease and slavery."

"An unfortunate turn of events," Wally said.

"Unfortunate? By 1600, 99 percent of the population had died of the diseases brought by Columbus and others. For those who didn't die right away, there was always slavery. Columbus thought that my people made great enslaved people," Lucy bellowed.

"Wally, I think we should table Columbus. Why bring that animosity and trouble here?" Al seemed to end the discussion, but Wally continued.

"I don't know if we can do that. I hear King Joseph's grandfather was Italian, and you know how temperamental the king can be."

"Betty, delete that immediately, or we're all in trouble."

Betty redacted Wally's statement and started to reword the statement when Lucy interrupted.

"In light of the massive genocide perpetrated on the native population, we are heartily recommending that any mention of Columbus be banned from the country of Matilda, which should be named Lucayos or Lukka-cairi."

"Betty, leave that in. It's Lucy's feelings, and King Joseph needs to hear what the native population thinks."

Jeremy changed the subject. "How about Martin Luther King Day and Juneteenth? Can we approve those?"

"Yeah, we should do that to appease our Black residents," Wally said in a sarcastic tone.

Al felt he had to reprimand Wally. "You really are a superb jerk. I will explain the history of Martin Luther King Day and Juneteenth, and then we can make rational decisions.

"Martin Luther King fought for civil rights with a non-violent method reminiscent of Mohandas Gandhi. His actions and speeches inspired many and moved the country closer to equality. After his assassination in 1968, the lawmakers started considering making his birthday a national holiday."

"They waited until after he died to *even* think about it?" Lucy said loudly. "What does that tell you?"

"That tells me that he gave the ultimate sacrifice, and therefore, it raised the level of his commitment," Al shot back.

"What about Juneteenth? I don't even really understand that one." Jeremy was trying to ease tensions.

Al was quick to answer. "Juneteenth is tied to the story of enslaved Black people in Galveston, Texas, learning that they had been emancipated, close to two and a half years after the Emancipation Proclamation had formally been put into place. So, it commemorates the end of racial chattel slavery."

"But no one in our little country of Matilda has ever been enslaved or, for that matter, enslaved anyone. Therefore, it is unimportant," Wally stated.

"You are so wrong, not to mention insensitive. Our population is made of so many people whose existence was affected," Al said.

"There should be a Taino Day, too," Lucy chimed in.

"And Lincoln!" Wally added.

Jeremy offered a compromise. "What if we just had a "Great People Day.' It could mean whatever anyone would want it to mean. Our citizens could celebrate who they thought important no matter which culture or history they thought most important."

"That's a great idea, Jeremy. If you want it to be Columbus Day, Martin Luther King Day, or....," Wally said.

"Hatuey Day?" Lucy interrupted. "He was a Taíno leader and the first prominent freedom fighter of the Americas. On February 2, 1512, he died at the hands of the European invaders because he tried to organize resistance."

"I would like to expand on Jeremy's idea. How about we also add a Great Events Day?" Al said, beaming.

"I like it," Jeremy said. Even Lucy gave a half smile.

"It could be Juneteenth, Fourth of July, or Guy Fawkes Day," Al said.

"Who the heck is that?" Wally scrunched up his face.

"A guy who tried to blow up Parliament and kill King James I in 1605. But that's the point, Wally. It's a big fireworks day in Britain because the plot was uncovered, and the king was saved. It may not mean anything to you, but there may be people in Matilda who would miss their fireworks on November 5."

"I think we are making progress. Betty, please read the holidays that we have."

"Great People Day, Great Event Day, Veterans Memorial Day, King Joseph's Day, Founding Day."

Everyone looked satisfied.

MEETING 4

Wally looked suspiciously at the sixteen-year-old girl who sat at the table. However, before he could speak, Lucy answered his question. "This is my half-sister, Maggie."

Al spoke up. "I invited Maggie because she was raised in America and represents an alternative view—also a younger view than her half-sister."

Al looked at Wally, Lucy, and Jeremy. They seemed to accept his rationale.

"Besides, I just came from a meeting with King Joseph. He wanted to know what we had come up with so far. He was so pleased with our idea of Great Persons Day and Great Event Day that he told me to add three religious holidays to the calendar."

"What three holidays?" asked Lucy.

"Any three that a person would like. If you are Christian, it could be Christmas and Easter. If you are Jewish, it could be Rosh Hosannah, Yom Kippur, or Purim," Al said.

"The Muslims could have their Eid al-Fitr and Eid al-Adha." Jeremy looked to Lucy to gauge her reaction.

"You might not call it a holiday, and we don't have a name for it," Lucy said. "For lack of a better word, many of us observe a sort of Un-Thanksgiving. Taino women dance to the spirit of Hatuey and ask for an answer from the *Great Mystery*. By the time the Pilgrims landed on Plymouth Rock, our race had already been written off as not existing."

"What a downer," Maggie moaned. "If you must wallow in the past, then create a 'Taino Day' and have the people celebrate what was good about our culture."

Lucy nodded.

"I think we're done here," Al pronounced.

"Didn't you mention that we could have nine holidays? By my count, we only have eight," Jeremy asked.

"You're correct," Al said. "I assumed that Thanksgiving would be the ninth. It is the most universally celebrated holiday in the USA."

Jeremy frowned. "In light of what Lucy revealed, it might not be a great idea for Matilda."

"We could have a fun holiday like Halloween or Valentine's Day," Maggie offered.

Al launched into an explanation. "Halloween is a perversion of the words 'All Hallows Eve.' The first day of November was considered the feast of All Saints, or as it was then called, All Holy or All Hallowed. The night before a holiday was also considered holy and celebrated.

"However, in ancient times, the Celtic people celebrated the same night as the night that 'the dark time of year' began. It was the end of the harvest, and they hoped they had enough food stored for the winter. This they observed with the pagan ritual of Samhain. To not drive away the pagans they were trying to keep Christian, the priests allowed the holiday to be tied to All Saints Day. It encouraged people to bake 'soul cakes' for lost souls who might not become saints. Poor people were given these cakes if they went door to door on Hallow Eve thus beginning..."

"Trick or treating," Jeremy said triumphantly.

"But what you are saying is that this has a religious background. Therefore, it falls under religious choices. Let's move on," Wally urged.

"Bah, humbug," Maggie jeered.

"Wrong holiday," Jeremy said.

"St. Valentine's Day celebrates an actual person who most Christian churches made a saint. However, it was never a national holiday anywhere," Al said.

"Then we can get rid of St. Valentine," Wally suggested.

"Maybe, but there is an interesting legend associated with Valentine."

"I want to hear it," Maggie said. "I love love."

"During the Roman Empire, the Emperor forbade soldiers to marry because it would make them soft. However, if a soldier wanted to marry, Valentine, a Christian priest, would secretly perform the ceremony. Eventually, he was found out and executed by the Romans. Thus began the tradition of him being the saint of lovers."

"Great story, but what does it have to do with our task of creating holidays?" groused Wally.

"It could be one of the people's choices for 'Great Persons Day," Jeremy said.

"How about this?" Al said. "St Valentine's Day stays an option for those that want it, but we create a new holiday that reflects the love of St. Valentine's Day, the gratitude of Thanksgiving, and the understanding of our diversity. We could call it Love, Appreciation, Thanks, and Enjoyment Day or the LATE holiday. It could be late in the year as a celebration of all we have accomplished socially, culturally, and economically."

"But too late in the year, and it would conflict with Christmas, which you know many are going to choose as a holiday," Jeremy noted.

"If you make it the third Thursday of November, it is just our version of Thanksgiving—and you know how my people feel about that," Lucy added.

"How about November 11? It could replace Veterans Day, which has been moved to May as Veterans Memorial Day?"

Al, Jeremy, Lucy, and Maggie looked at a makeshift calendar they had created.

"It works," Jeremy observed.

"C'mon, Wally, what do you say we make it unanimous?" Al pleaded as they looked to the last member of the group.

"Okay, I'm in as long as you mention to the king how instrumental I was in creating this calendar of holidays."

"Betty," Al said with a smile, "Come join us for a toast. As our youngest Maggie, would you do the honor?"

They raised their glasses of water as Maggie led them in a toast. "To LATE Day, love, appreciation, thanks, and hopefully some fine entertainment.

CONTRIBUTORS

Perhaps best known as the lead singer of Twisted Sister, Dee Snider is also an accomplished songwriter, screenwriter (feature film *My Enemy's Enemy*, children's animated series *Monsters Rock*) and author (novel *Frats*, memoir *Shut Up and Give Me the Mic*). His songwriting credits include "Magic of Christmas Day" recorded by Celine Dion. Dee has starred in reality TV shows, including *Celebrity Apprentice, Gone Country, Rock the Cradle, Growing Up Twisted, Celebrity Wife Swap,* and *Masked Singer* and is a sought-after voiceover artist. His nationally syndicated radio show, *House of Hair,* airs on 250 stations. Dee also starred in the Tony-award winning musical *Rock of Ages* and wrote the lyrics, music and book for *A Rock 'n' Roll Christmas Tale.*

Suzanne Kamata first came to Japan in 1988 to teach English on the government-sponsored JET Program and wound up staying. She has now lived in Tokushima Prefecture for well over half of her life. She is the author of several books based on her experiences including the novel *The Baseball Widow* (Wyatt-Mackenzie Publishing, 2021), which won an IPPY Award, and the middle-grade novel *Pop Flies, Robo-pets and Other Disasters* (One Elm Books, 2020).

Merav Fima holds a PhD in Creative Writing from Monash University in Melbourne, Australia. Her prose and poetry have appeared in a number of anthologies and literary journals, including: *Parchment: A Journal of Contemporary Canadian Jewish Writing*; *Poetica Magazine*; and *Meanjin Quarterly*. Her short story, 'Bride Immaculate', won the 2014 Energheia Literary Competition (Matera, Italy) and 'Rose among the Thorns' was a finalist in the *Tiferet* literary journal's 2019 fiction contest.

Matt McGee is a six-time Pushcart Prize nominee who writes in the Los Angeles area. His novel *Hungry* is available on Amazon.

Farouk Gulsara writes prescriptions by day and nonsense by night. The author of two non-fiction books, *Inside the Twisted Mind of Rifle Range Boy* and *Real Lessons from Reel Life*, he writes regularly on his blog *Rifle Range Boy*. Occasionally, the muse teases him to churn out creative writing. His works have appeared in *Borderless, Men Matters* and *Eastlit* literary journals and the anthologies *Best Asian Short Stories 2017* and *Bitter Root Sweet Fruit*.

Rebecca Rush is a writer and comic from the East Coast living in Los Angeles. Her words have appeared in numerous outlets, including *Psychology Today*, *Fodor's Travel*, and *Huffington Post*. Her essay "I've Been Swindled" was recently released in the anthology *Red Flags: Tales of Love & Instinct* from Running Wild Press. She holds a B.A. in English

Literature with a concentration in Creative Writing from the University of Connecticut. @RebeccaRush639 on socials. #ActuallyAutistic

---

Kwasi Shade represents the true myriad of Caribbean dichotomies in their stories, testing the parameters of Creole vernacular and communicating the Carnival Aesthetic. They have participated in the Cropper Foundation Writers' Workshop, Trinidad and Tobago Film Festival's Screenwriters' Workshop with the Canadian High Commission, Studio Museum in Harlem Museum Education Practicum, NYI Global Institute of Cultural, Cognitive and Linguistic Studies and Monique & Kei's writers' retreat. Their work has been exhibited at the Kirschmann Gallery, New Orleans; Alice Yard and Granderson Lab, both in Trinidad; Nuit Rose and the Carifesta Exhibition, Trinidad National Museum. Their poetry, short stories and drawings have appeared in *Pree Lit*, *Moko*, *Enby*, *Tamarind*, *Pinkwashed*, *Prismatica*, and *Culturego*.

When Meredith Dylan is not running around with her teenage daughters, she can be found immersed in a good book or singing very badly to Broadway musicals. With a background in journalism and advertising and a career in merchandising, she put her writing goals on hold to raise her family. She is currently working on her first romance novel series. She lives in Long Island, New York, with her husband, her girls and their cat Jelly.

Sheerin Shahab is an introvert who prefers a book over company any day. Hence, she is a reader, a nature lover, and a die-hard chai fan. She loves to read and write short stories. Several of her stories have appeared in anthologies published by The Hive Publishers and Writefluence. You can find her stories and poems at https://penmancy.com/author/sheerin-shahab/ and on her Facebook page, Alfaaz-e-Sheerin.

Cynthia Gallaher, a Chicago-based poet, is the author of four poetry collections, including *Epicurean Ecstasy: More Poems About Food, Drink, Herbs and Spices*, and three chapbooks, including *Drenched*. Her award-winning nonfiction/memoir/creativity guide is *Frugal Poets' Guide to Life: How to Live a Poetic Life, Even If You Aren't a Poet*. One of her poems will be sent on NASA's flight to the Moon's South Pole later this decade.

Shai Afsai lives in Providence, Rhode Island. Enough said.

John Grey is an Australian poet and short story writer who resides in the United States. His works have been most recently published in *Stand, Santa Fe Literary Review*, and *Sheepshead Review* and are forthcoming in *McNeese Review, La Presa* and *California Quarterly*. His latest books, *Between Two Fires, Covert, Memory Outside the Head* and *Between Two Fires,* are available through Amazon.

Evie Groch, Ed.D., is a Field Supervisor/Mentor for new administrators in graduate schools of education. Her opinion pieces, humor, poems, short stories, memoir vignettes, and other articles have been published in the *New York Times, San Francisco Chronicle,* and *Contra Costa Times,* as well as in anthologies and many online outlets. The themes of travel, language, immigration, and justice are special for her since she herself is an immigrant who speaks several languages.

Kaja Weeks is a poet, essayist, and classically trained singer. Her writing, which has earned two Pushcart Prize nominations, has appeared in *The Sugar House Review, Ars Medica: A Journal of Medicine, The Arts and Humanities, Under the Gum Tree, Brevity Blog* and elsewhere. Kaja's memoir-based chapbook, *Mouth Quill—Poems with Ancestral Roots,* was published in 2020. An alumnus of New Directions, a post-graduate writing program of The Washington-Baltimore Center for Psychoanalysis, Kaja's literary website is www.-lyricovertones.com.

Perin Marolia took up librarianship as her profession, and has a Master's degree and a Doctorate in Library and Information Science. For the greater part of her career, she taught Library and Information Science at university level. She lives in Mumbai, India, with her husband. She has two daughters, one of whom is married and has appointed Perin as honorary babysitter for her two-year-old son.

Jasmine Tritten is an award-winning author born in Denmark. She has written numerous short stories that have been published in various anthologies. In 2015 she published *The Journey of an Adventuresome Dane*. With her husband, she also wrote and illustrated a children's story *Kato's Grand Adventure*, which was published in 2018. Jasmine also wrote, illustrated, and published a travel memoir, *On the Nile with a Dancing Dane* in 2020. She resides in enchanting Corrales, New Mexico, with her husband and two cats.

A. Shydian is a third-generation Armenian American who lives in Central Oregon with her husband and daughter. After graduating with an advanced degree in history, she moved back to Oregon and began researching her family roots. Now a business owner and historian, she continues research into her family while helping others with genealogy projects. Shydian is her maternal great-grandmother's maiden name, one that has been both difficult and rewarding to research.

Anita Haas is a differently-abled Canadian writer and teacher based in Spain. She has published books on film and flamenco (with her husband, Carlos Aguilar), two novelettes, a short story collection, and articles, poems and fiction in both English and Spanish. Her most recent work is the bilingual picture book, *Chato, the Puppy-Cat/Chato, el Perri-Gato*, which she wrote, translated, and illustrated. Proceeds from the sales are being donated to local animal shelters.

William John Rostron is the author of a series of novels set in the world of modern music and culture, *Band in the Wind, Sound of Redemption,* and *Brotherhood of Forever* have received critical acclaim from Writers Digest and the Online Book Club Review, as well as the standalone novel, *The Other Side of the Wind*. He has published over three dozen short stories in anthologies, five receiving awards from Writers Digest. Most of these pieces appear in his short story compilation, *A Flamingo Under the Carousel*. Five of his stories have been produced on the New York stage. www.WilliamJohnRostron.com

About the Editor

Christina Hoag was slated to enter the world in Zambia but made her grand debut in New Zealand. Three weeks later, she moved to Fiji, the first of seven countries she grew up in. As an adult, she lived in three other countries. A former journalist for the Miami Herald and Associated Press, she reported from more than a dozen countries in Latin America for *Time, Business Week, The New York Times, Financial Times,* and *Sunday Times* among other media. She is the author of novels *Law of the Jungle, The Blood Room, Girl on the Brink,* named as Suspense Magazine's Best of YA, and *Skin of Tattoos,* a Silver Falchion award finalist. She is also the co-author of *Peace in the Hood: Working with Gang Members to End the Violence* (Turner). Her short stories and essays have appeared in numerous literary reviews including *Other Side of Hope, Lunch Ticket, Toasted Cheese* and *Shooter,* and have won several awards. More information about her is available on https://christina-hoag.com.